Cam's Chance
Arrowtown Book 5
By Lisa Oliver

Cam's Chance (Arrowtown #5)

Cover Design by Lisa Oliver

Background and model images purchased from Shutterstock.com.

First Edition November 2019

Cam's Chance is a work of fiction. Names, characters, places and incidents are either the product of the author's imagination or are used fictitiously and any resemblance to any actual persons, living or dead, events or locales is entirely coincidental.

Table of Contents

Dedication

To Amanda and Carla – as always, you lovely ladies make my words shine.

For the rest of you who are reading this – yes, I am talking to you personally – please remember how amazing you are, how you have more strength than you know, and how wonderful my world is with you in it. Thank you from the bottom of my heart.

Chapter One

"I don't want to hear about it. I'm not coming back!" Cam looked up, making sure the door to his office was firmly closed, before turning his attention back to the phone. "We've been through this a million times. I don't care how much money you offer me..."

Cam frowned at his screen as a hissed amount came through.

"What the hell are you smoking? You don't have that kind of money for a government contract."

He raised his eyebrows as the voice on the other end of the phone spoke quickly.

"Oh, I see. It's a private job. Your circumstances have changed now that your old man is dead. How sweet. You finally got your hands on all his money. Lord knows that's all you're ever concerned about. I'm still not interested."

The voice on the other end rose in annoyance.

Cam had had enough. "No, you listen to me. We had a deal. You swore you would lose my number. I've cleaned up your messes a dozen times and after the shit that went down last time... NO. Stop right there," he added as the voice tried to interrupt. "People died. My friends died. I'm not letting that shit happen again."

The tone on the other end of the call went soft, cajoling, and Cam heaved a huge sigh. "There's no point in trying to con me with that shit either, Austin. Threats and seductions just don't work for me, and besides, I've seen your dick. I wasn't impressed. You'd fuck a rattle snake if doing so meant you'd get your own way. Now, there's a thought. How about you do that. But leave me out of it."

Tapping the screen to end the call was never as satisfying as slamming down a phone receiver, but it would have to do. Leaning back in his chair, Cam ran his hands through the bristles on his head. After months of letting his hair and beard grow, he'd finally shaved it all off, head and face. He felt strangely naked without it all. But Arrowtown was in the middle of a heat wave, and since some stupid bear shifter had grabbed his hair the week before in an attempt to stop himself being thrown out, Cam decided some stringent personal grooming was in order.

"Fates save me from idiots and stupid people," he muttered, his mind still on the call as he heard a knock on his office door. Righting himself in his chair, he looked down at the papers covering his desk, before calling out, "enter." Looking up, he saw it was

Darwin, an ex-stripper who was now one of his better bartenders. "What's up?"

"Nothing much." Darwin bounced in, flopping in the nearest chair. "The bar's quiet. Just the locals in. Everything's stocked for the evening crowd. I just came in to see if you wanted anything to eat, before I headed off for the night."

"How are the little ones doing?" Cam had been as shocked as anyone else when Simon, Darwin's mate gave birth to twins, in his shifted form no less. Even the Doc was sure Simon's shift would kill the little ones, as it usually did with any non-furry shifter males who could give birth. But no. It seemed Simon's snake form was the only way a male of his kind could give birth and the twins had been running Darwin and Simon ragged ever since.

"They're walking, already. Can you believe it?" Darwin ran his hand over his forehead. "I swear the only peace I get is when I come in here."

Cam hid his smirk by rubbing under his nose. "You know, if you're ever getting too tired and want some time off..."

"No. No." Darwin shook his head quickly. Then he groaned. "Gods, doesn't that make me sound like a horrible parent? But Simon is just so calm and good with them. Throw up, tantrums, teething, and that's all times two because of course those little darlings do everything together. Simon just takes it all in his stride. I swear that man's a saint in a snake skin."

"He has the added benefit of being able to work from home most times," Cam agreed. "But the offer's there. I'm sure I can get Nicky or Sue to cover for you if you want to spend more time bonding with Sebastian and Thomas."

"I do bond with them," Darwin said with a glower. "The last time I ended up covered in glue and a million shades of glitter. It took me a week to get it all out of my hair."

"I did wonder if you were trying out a new look." Cam let his grin show this time. "But no, thank you. I grabbed a sandwich earlier. Everything is all quiet in here. I can run the bar until Nicky comes in. You head off home and enjoy some quality family time."

Darwin pushed himself out of his chair. "I adore my twins with everything I have and would die for them in a heartbeat. But I swear, if I don't get some quality Simon time soon, I'm not going to be responsible for my behavior."

Cam's grin widened. "Sounds like you need to get laid. That might improve your mood. Why don't you get Seth to babysit for a night? I'm sure he could handle two extra little ones for one night."

"Hmm, that could be an idea. We haven't done that for a while." Darwin's smile was a lot lighter now. "Yeah, I'll do that. See if I can't drag that man of mine out for a good meal and a night of passion. Could be fun."

Sauntering over to the door, Darwin turned just as he opened it. "Hey, did you see a new bakery opened up in town? Just next to Mrs. Hooper's store. The smells coming out of that place are amazing. Could be an idea to put in an order – see if they want to supply us with lunches now that Mary's handed in her notice. I know you tried Hazel at the diner, but she's already too busy with her own business. This place is new, and you still haven't got the catering ordered for Mary's going away do."

"Shit, I'd forgotten about that." Cam rustled through his papers. "When's Mary leaving again?"

"Friday." Darwin chuckled. "I've already organized her gift and charged it to the bar. The rest of the staff are coming in Friday lunch for her farewell. I mentioned the bakery because I thought it might be an idea to call them and see if they can cater for say fifty people at short notice. Think of it like a sort of job interview for them."

"Well, we can't have Mary cooking on her last day, can we." Cam gave up on his papers and reached for his phone. "I'll call Mrs. Hooper and get the bakery number. Go on. You've done your bit. Get home to your twins."

"I'm calling Seth first. You call the bakery pronto and then get your ass out to the bar. Dave Hooper is in with his cronies. You know what they get like when their glasses are empty." Darwin nodded as he left, closing the door quietly behind him.

"I thought Mrs. Hooper had that old fart on a drink budget," Cam grumbled even though Darwin had gone. But the young mouse shifter was right. Dave Hooper should be his first priority. Pocketing his phone, Cam got up, stepping around his cluttered desk and headed out to the bar. He could make his call after he'd made sure Dave wasn't helping himself. The last thing he wanted on a quiet weekday afternoon was to deal with a drunk buffalo shifter on a bender – or Mrs. Hooper's wrath if he let it happen.

/~/~/~/~/

Fergus was in the process of transferring a huge tray of buns from the oven to the bench top when the phone rang. Without missing a beat, he slid the bun tray onto the counter, and reached over to swipe up the phone. "Arrowtown Bakery. What delectable delights can the Fabulous Fergus send your way today?"

A cough sounded on the other end and then a deep chuckle sent shivers down Fergus's spine. "Fabulous Fergus, ha?" The chuckle was still there. "Well this is the not-so-fabulous Cam, from the bar at the end of the main street. I don't think we've met."

"Er... Yes, no." Fergus wanted to fan himself. *That voice! Makes my insides all mushy.* "I mean, I've seen the bar obviously, but I haven't had a chance to call in and introduce myself yet. Bakery hours are the opposite of yours, I reckon."

"Hmm, they probably are."

What is this man? He sounds better than a double chocolate chip cookie smothered in chocolate sauce.

"Anyhow, I wanted to talk to you about the delectable delights you're promising," Cam continued.

Me, on a platter, covered in chocolate and strawberries. "Yes." Fergus's voice squeaked and he cleared his throat and tried for a deeper tone. "I mean, yes, of course, how can we help you today? I was told you have a fully functioning kitchen." Fergus knew, because Mrs Hooper, who'd rented him his space, told him the bar and the local diner were his only other competition in town and that they stuck to home-cooked basics instead of pastries and breads.

"We do have a kitchen, yes," Cam seemed pleased Fergus knew that much. "But my bartender Darwin was suitably impressed with the smells coming from your establishment, he recommended you for the catering of a lunch we're giving on Friday for one of our staff who's leaving. You could think of it as a prelude to future business opportunities if it helps."

Helps what? The bakery had only been open two weeks, but already Fergus was seeing a profit. However, he didn't have it in him to alienate one of the longest running businesses in his new town. It just wasn't in his nature. "That is very sweet of you to think of helping me. I'm sure we'll have plenty to discuss after the luncheon. Can you tell me, how many people, shifter types expected, and so on?"

Fergus listened with half an ear, scribbling down details, his mind already planning what he'd have to do to fill such a large order, while still keeping his fledgling business stocked, all on such short notice. He was going to be working until midnight just to keep up. He only came out of his business mindset when Cam said, "I'll look forward to meeting you on Friday."

"What?" Fergus dropped his pencil. Bending down, he clipped the side of his head on the counter. "No, no, I won't be there. Someone has to keep the ovens burning here, you know. But you have my assurance, my staff will be there at eleven thirty on Friday. They will set up, serve, and clear everything away afterwards. Thank you so much for your business. Have a fantabulous day."

Dropping the phone on the counter, Fergus sprawled across it, letting out a long sigh. His whole body thrummed, and that was just from hearing Cam's voice. *I am in so much trouble,* he thought, vowing he would avoid the enigmatic Cam as much as possible. The last thing he wanted as a new business owner was to be seen as an easy lay.

"Boss, boss?" Sarah, his assistant came running in and gasped seeing him prone across the counter. "What's wrong? I heard you groaning."

"Did I groan?" Fergus turned his head and eyed his new friend from the counter. "Of course, you heard me with your cute little bunny ears. I can assure you, any noise coming from my lips wasn't intentional." He sighed as he pushed himself upright again. "We have an order. A big catering job for Friday and I need..."

"Oh, who is it for? Where?" Sarah grabbed one of the fresh buns off the tray and started pulling bits off and nibbling them. "Wow, these taste so good. I'm so glad I'm a shifter and run around a lot, or I'd weigh a ton working here."

"I weigh a ton in my shifted form anyway," Fergus picked up a bun of his own. "Now, where was I? Oh yes, So Cam called, from the bar…" He trailed off expectantly and Sarah didn't disappoint.

"Oh, my gods, you talked to Cam? Isn't he dreamy?" Clasping her bun in her hands, Sarah sighed. "But he doesn't look at little bunnies like me. He's got that, 'I'm a big tough military man' type vibe going on, and oh, but he's so sweet too. Like when Doc needed a scanning machine for the pregnant people, he had a fundraising night, and they raised heaps of money. Of, course that was the night the sheriff raided the bar – not the new sheriff but the old one and then…"

"Are you telling tales out of school, Sarah?" Deputy Joe's head peered around the door. "I came in for a coffee and to see if you had any of those white chocolate and raspberry muffins left, but there was no one at the counter."

"Joe." Fergus beamed. He'd taken a liking to the big buffalo shifter the moment he saw him. Even though Joe was actually checking him out for security purposes, making sure Fergus wasn't one of his long distant relatives, the two men got on from day one. "I put your muffin aside for you, figuring you'd be in. How's your adorably grouchy other half? And those equally adorable twins of yours?"

"Petra is babbling every waking moment, and Finch seems to love listening to her. As for Doc, he's just as grouchy, but I'd never want him to change." Deputy Joe stepped in twirling his hat on his finger. "Did I hear you talking about Cam over at the bar?"

"He's so dreamy," Sarah said with another sigh. Her bun was almost gone. "And oh, he called, and he gave Fergus a big order. Isn't that wonderful?"

"That'll be for Mary's going away party, I reckon," Joe said with a smile. "That could be regular business for you, if you can get it Fergus. You'll have to wow him with your muffins."

"I wow everyone just by walking down the street," Fergus said with a toss of his hair, but he grinned to show he was teasing. "Okay, so we absolutely have to make sure the order is our best yet. I need to tempt Cam's taste buds. What type of shifter is he?"

Joe tapped the side of his nose and shook his head. "No one knows, but he's the only one of his kind in this town. I do know he can make a bear, a wolf, or a lion nervous, so don't get on the wrong side of him."

I'd far rather be under him, calling his name, Fergus thought with a sigh. Shaking off any sexy thoughts, because that really wasn't appropriate in his spotless kitchen, he grabbed a piece of paper and started planning a menu to wow the man with the spine-tingling voice.

Chapter Two

Cam stood near the back of the bar, keeping a wary eye on things as staff and locals alike made the most of Mary's going away party. Mary, a cute lioness with a sassy nature and a strong right hook, had met her mate not ten feet from where Cam was standing. Now, her belly had swollen so big she could barely see her toes and her mate had finally put his foot down and insisted she give up her work so she could stay home and prepare for the litter they were expecting.

Rubbing his chest, Cam ignored the way his errant thoughts of family and litters tinged the corner of his brain and poured himself a large whiskey. He never got drunk but having a glass in hand was a good way of stopping him reaching for his phone. Ever since hearing 'Fabulous Fergus's' voice three days before, Cam couldn't stop thinking about the man and that was unusual enough to bother him.

His affairs, if they could be called that, lasted from five to twenty minutes long depending on how urgent his need and how well a person moved. He made a point of never fucking anyone who lived in town, although his office desk at the back of the bar saw a bit of action from visitors moving through town. But the operative word was 'through'. Cam never thought twice about a person after his cock was tucked back in his pants again, and he made sure to only scratch an itch with people who had the same attitude.

Fabulous Fergus broke all Cam's rules. For one thing, Cam was thinking about him and they hadn't even met. And if Cam had his way, they weren't likely too. The wonderful food notwithstanding, Fergus lived in town. He was a permanent resident and new business owner. *Off limits in other words.*

Cam managed a half smile as Mayor Ra stepped up to the bar, holding an empty bottle and an equally empty glass. "It was nice of you to come down here just to say goodbye to Mary," he said, putting down his own drink so he could replenish Ra's.

"She's a good lady and that mate of hers is a fine young man," Ra said with a shrug. "Besides, I heard you got Fergus to do the catering and I can't resist his eclairs. Have you tasted them?"

No. Cam couldn't bring himself to taste any of the delicious food being served by three very friendly bunny shifters. He just knew if the food tasted as good as it smelled, then he'd be lurking around the bakery door at some ungodly hour of the morning just to get another taste. "I've been busy," he said, because all shifters could smell a lie. "The crowd seem happy with it all though."

"Fergus runs a good clean business. Seems like a genuine guy." Ra nodded. "I had Deputy Joe check him out of course, but it turns out he's not a buffalo like Joe's relatives, but a genuine Highland bull shifter. He's turned out to be a godsend in one respect. If I hear my wee Seth is having a frazzled day with the kiddies, I grab six of the cream donuts Fergus makes and my mate is happy again."

For a tiger shifter, and ruling mayor, Ra was ridiculously smitten with his bunny mate, although even Cam could admit young Seth was adorable. "So, Fergus hasn't been here long then?" Okay. Cam would admit it to himself, he was curious about his mental obsession. He grabbed Ra another bottle of his favorite beer and poured a soda for Seth in a fresh glass.

Leaning his elbows on the bar counter, Ra seemed happy enough to talk. "He came in on a transfer from another shifter town up north about six weeks ago," he said, tilting up the bottle and taking a long swig. "He filed a business plan along with his application to live here. Bank statements showed he had enough money to buy his house here, and start up his business, at least according to Simon. Rocky called the sheriff at his old town, but apparently, he hadn't had any troubles there. According to his application, Fergus just wanted a change of scenery and warmer weather, and he said the same thing when I spoke to him."

"Hmm." Cam pushed Seth's new drink across the counter.

He was feeling surprisingly put out and he wasn't sure if it was his spidey senses warning him about an unknown man who just appeared in town out of nowhere for flimsy reasons, or if he didn't like the fact Ra had spoken to the man when he hadn't. "He'll find it plenty warm enough here until winter hits again."

"Seriously, you should hire him to do your lunches," Ra said with his laid-back grin. He leaned further over the counter and whispered, "don't tell Mary, but his buns and salads, sandwiches, and pies are a lot better than hers. He makes all his own bread and pastries and anything I've eaten of his just melts in my mouth."

"Oh yeah," Cam laughed. "I'll be sure to tell a heavily pregnant lioness that someone else in town bakes better than she does. In fact, why don't I call her over and you can tell her yourself."

"You keep your big mouth shut." Ra's face went white. Snatching up the drinks he ordered, he disappeared into the crowd. Still chuckling, Cam filled a few more drink orders and was just going to grab some empty glasses when he spotted Sarah, a young bunny shifter who'd come from the bakery, lurking at the side of the counter.

"What's up, Sarah? No one giving you any trouble, are they?" Cam picked up a rag and started cleaning down the counter top.

"Oh no. Everyone is always lovely to me." Sarah perked up at being spoken to directly. Cam was well aware she harbored a crush on him, but he made a point of never encouraging it. "I just wondered, or rather the boss wondered, well... did you like the food?" The last bit came out as a rush.

"Look at all the people around you," Cam said, waving his rag to show the crowd who all seemed very happy snatching up the remains of the huge lunch Fergus had sent over. "Not an unhappy face in the lot. You can tell your boss I'm very pleased."

"He'll be pleased you're pleased." Sarah hopped on one foot to the other. "It's just… what about you? Did you have anything to eat from what the boss sent over?"

What the hell? Cam's spidey senses went into overdrive and his concern about the mysterious Fergus increased. "No," he snapped, far harsher than intended. "I don't eat cakes and sweets and I had a big breakfast before I started today. But if all your boss is interested in, is getting compliments from me, then he can forget it. I'm not the type to hold someone's hand and tell them how good they are at what they do. I just expect them to get on with it. Now, if you'll excuse me," because Sarah seemed close to tears, "I have work to do." He strode out of the bar, heading for his office. He'd behaved like an asshole, and he'd find a way to make it up to Sarah later, but for now he had some calls to make. If the self-proclaimed Fabulous Fergus was up to no good, he'd know about it before nightfall.

/~/~/~/~/

"Aww, sweetie, come here." Fergus folded the weeping Sarah into his arms, patting her hair and crooning softly. His three young staff had come back with empty platters full of the praises everyone gave for the food. Only Sarah seemed upset, and Fergus was quick to send the other two home with a wad of cash each, so he could talk to Sarah in private. "It's okay. You tell the best boss in the world who upset you and I'll go and stuff his face with lamingtons and then stomp on them."

"Lamingtons? What's that?" Just as he intended, Sarah was diverted from whoever upset her.

"A rather delicious sponge cake actually," Fergus said very seriously, "covered in either a chocolate or strawberry sauce and then it's covered in coconut which is honestly quite yummy. They're made in Australia and New Zealand."

"Well, they'd be wasted on Cam." Sarah sniffed and swiped at the tears on her cheeks. "I didn't do anything bad. I only asked him if he liked the food and he said everyone there were all happy with it."

"I can tell they enjoyed it all," Fergus eyed the empty trays and pans littering his counter top. "I'm not sure there was a crumb left of anything. So come on, if this Cam person was so happy with the catering, then what did he say to upset you?"

Sarah's face went bright red. "I might have got a teensy bit pushy," she admitted holding up her fingers to show a tiny amount. "It's just, I thought you might have liked him, and then I thought well if I could come back and tell you how much he loved your cooking, then maybe you would go and meet him and it would be so romantic."

Fergus forced a smile on his face, even though his heart plummeted. "And I take it, instead of your dreams of a happy ever after, he told you he hated the food and wouldn't date me on a bet, am I right?"

"I never said anything about dating," Sarah protested. Then she slumped. "He said he doesn't eat cakes and sweet things, and that he'd had a big breakfast. I mean, how ridiculous is that, not eating cakes or sweets."

"Maybe he has a sugar allergy we don't know about snookums." Inside, Fergus was trying to work out why the staunch bar owner wouldn't eat his food. Did he think it was poisoned or something?

"If he had a sugar allergy, he couldn't have alcohol either," Sarah said hotly. "And he was drinking at lunch time!"

"A lot of people do, sweetness." Fergus wasn't sure what to make of Cam's notions either, but then he didn't know the man, so he wasn't sure it mattered. "The thing is, whatever he said, it doesn't matter." He gripped Sarah's shoulders loosely and smiled.

"Remember, we are fabulous, amazing and spread happiness and cheer wherever we go, right?"

"That's why you employed me." Sarah stood up straighter. "Because I'm Sensational Sarah."

"So, we'll forget about the grouchy bar owner, and you'll trot yourself out to the cabinet and help yourself to a raspberry éclair. I need to know if they have the right balance of sweet and tart. Can you do that for me?"

"It's why you hired me." Sarah skipped out of the kitchen, and then she leaned her head back around the door frame. "You really are the best boss, did you know that?"

"But of course, although I thank you for telling me. Now get along." Fergus made shooing motions with his hands; his smile fixed in place until he knew Sarah was distracted in the front of the shop. Tipping a large amount of dough out of a steel bowl, Fergus lightly coated the counter top with flour and started to punch the air out of the proven lump.

Damn man, upsetting Sarah like that. Thump. Thump. *There's no need for anyone to be so hurtful.* Thump. Thump. Thump. *I've a good mind to... no. no. no.* Fergus refused to let himself get angry. If anything, he reminded himself, he should feel sorry for Cam who clearly had never appreciated how happy a perfectly baked pastry or cake could make someone feel.

He probably has issues, issues we know nothing about, Fergus thought, as he continued to work the dough under his hands. *Remember, if a person makes you feel bad, it's not usually got anything to do with what you did at all. Yes.*

Fergus was decided. He would put Cam's nasty tone to Sarah out of his head. From all accounts, Cam was well liked in town and had stuck up for smaller shifters more than once. *He's not a bully, he's just having a bad day.* And if Fergus's hot dreams of being taken by the man with the wonderful voice deflated along with his dough, then Fergus would live with that too. It wouldn't have been the first time he'd been disappointed.

Chapter Three

"Nothing." Cam glared at the piles of paper on his desk, then up at his computer screen. "Absolutely fucking nothing." Which wasn't strictly true but might well have been as far as Cam was concerned. He was looking for dirt. What he'd found was a swathe of useless information on Fabulous Fergus, from the make and registration of his car – a 1997 Jeep Cherokee four door sport, 4WD, in black - down to his graduation picture when Fergus completed his studies at the John Lawrence School of Bakery in 1999. Cam found awards in Fergus's name for sports and bakery; he'd scrolled through pictures of the man's family and siblings, although there was nothing of Fergus with his family after he turned eighteen. The man covered his social media accounts with snapshots of delicious foods and 'be happy' pictures, but of his actual life there was nothing.

No relationships. No messy breakups. No brushes with the law. Not even a speeding ticket. Extensive searches through police databases, shifter and human, had come up with nothing. Cam had made the calls he'd promised himself, and so far, nothing had come back from them either. Cam's teeth were grinding against each other, he was so antsy. *It's not possible for a man to be so squeaky clean.*

The phone rang. Cam glanced at it and seeing it was a withheld number, picked it up. Withheld usually meant a call from his type of people. "What have you got for me?"

"A little bird told me you're looking for someone, you naughty, naughty boy. Why didn't you call me?"

Cam cringed as he recognized the voice. "Austin, I thought I told you to lose my number."

"Aww, now why would I do that, when we make such a perfect team. I pay you money and you kill people for me."

"Not anymore I don't, and I haven't done for fucking years. I told you the last time was the final one, but it seems you're too stupid to remember our agreement."

"Now, don't be like that." Austin's laugh was like claws on a chalkboard – grating against every one of Cam's nerves. "I need you to do a job for me, and in return I have a file on a Mr. Fergus Franklin Ferdinand. I can even give you his most current address."

Cam bit back his response. He already had Fergus's address. The man lived two blocks away from where he did, although Austin had no way of knowing that.

"I have to say," Cam could hear the sound of Austin flicking through papers, "I can't for the life of me think why you want to hunt down this individual. The man is so clean he squeaks. My gods, did you see all those affirmation platitudes he posts on social media? What on earth would a do-gooder baker like Mr. Ferdinand be doing to attract your attention?"

"It's none of your business, is it?" Cam snarled across the phone lines. "I told you to stop calling me."

"Why would I stop calling, when you're the only one who can meet my *needs*." The last word was purred, and Cam felt his stomach churn. He knew exactly what needs Austin was talking about, and they were definitely not of the pleasurable variety. "It's only this one last job," Austin said happily. "Just one more, and I'll forget you ever existed, and you can have this file as a bonus."

"You gave me your word you'd lose my number after the last fiasco you sent me into." Cam was ready to throw his phone against the wall. "Now, fuck off. I've got work to do."

"Hmm, so I see. Tracking down the squeaky-clean Mr. Ferdinand. Such a curious person for you to waste your precious time and energies on. I can't help but be curious myself. So, are you going to tell me what Mr. Do-gooder did to pique your interest?" Austin's gasp was theatrically faked. "I know. I'll ask him myself, shall I. It's not a problem to send one of my men to the hick town he's living in and encourage him to come back here. Who knows, I might even ask him to bake me a cake, he could bring it along with him. Won't that be nice?

Tea and cake, and we can sit and chat about you."

"You leave him alone! He's got nothing to do with you or me!"

"Oh, but I think he must have something special to become the focus of your little investigation. No one puts in requests to the military and alphabet agencies for information about a nobody, now do they? Don't you worry. I'll take care of that little problem for you, and then you can take care of one for me. I'll be in touch when I've got results to share. Bye."

"NO!" Cam roared but it was too late. The 'call ended' sign flashed up on the screen before it went dark. Dropping his phone on the desk, Cam tugged at his non-existent hair. *Fuck, what the hell have I done? What if I was wrong? What if there genuinely isn't anything remotely suspicious about Fergus? What if he is who he presents himself to be? A sweet helpful, nice guy who makes delicious cakes for a living. Fuck. Fuck. Fuck. What the hell am I going to do now?*

Austin wasn't anyone to muck around with. Cam worked with him for years before realizing what an absolute shit the man could be to those who showed him loyalty. Known among underground sources as the Reckless Rhino who relished using shifters for their sharper physical attributes, Austin had an entitlement complex a mile wide and the authority to make most men quake in their boots.

The agency Austin ran was so deep undercover, no one could ever touch the man, but his lack of compassion for the suffering of anyone, human or shifter, was only revealed to Cam when the mission he was on with three others went to shit. No back up. No resources, at least that's what he was told at the time, and when Cam tried to fight for the friends he'd lost, he was told he was suffering from fatigue and ordered to rest.

He never went back. Cam used his leave time to work out his release from the military, and when Austin called him six months later for another job, he took great pleasure in telling the man where he could shove it. Cam believed at the time, he and Austin had an agreement. He would drop the matter of getting compensation for the lost men's family from the government, if Austin forgot he existed. It was a simple matter for Cam to help out the families himself through anonymous direct payments.

But Austin never forgot, keeping in touch at least once a year, dangling another job and even higher pay rates that Cam found easy to ignore. He was a petty nuisance, an annoyance, and as Cam was confident Austin had no idea where he was, he'd gotten comfortable. *And now look where it's gotten me. Fuck, poor Fergus.*

Cam only dithered for a second. He had first-hand knowledge about what happened to people who went for "a chat" with Austin. They were never heard from again, or worse they were found so badly injured they couldn't remember their own name. Shifters, humans, any type of paranormal, Austin didn't care. Insults bounced off his inch-thick skin, and he still plowed ahead, getting what he wanted anyway.

I could do the job for him. But Cam was already shaking his head. If he let Austin get his way once, the man would never stop and Cam's life, as he had it now, would be over.

As soon as Austin thought he had a hold over Cam, no matter what it was, he'd exploit it and use it until Cam was dead.

And Cam wasn't about to let that happen. Now all he had to do was protect Fergus, the young baker he'd never met, but who he knew everything about, without letting the man know the dire situation Cam's brainless actions had gotten him into.

Chapter Four

Fergus trudged up the pathway to his new home, his feet aching and his back sore. It was already dark, but after the catering job he'd done for the pub, Fergus knew his best way of getting any rest at all was to make sure the cabinets were filled for the Saturday morning crowd and then take the weekend off for himself. The Sensational Sarah was going to handle the till along with her brother Terrific Tommy. After his little pep talk, Sarah was determined to show she could handle the place herself, and as the shop was only open for four hours on a Saturday and Mrs. Hooper was right next door, Fergus trust she could do it.

Thumping up his porch steps, Fergus sighed. He'd been at work the best part of twenty hours and all he wanted was a hot shower, a cold drink, and the chance to put his feet up. Netflix was calling his name, and Fergus wasn't going to let anything interrupt his binge watching of *Sugar Rush*. "Home sweet home," he sang quietly, conscious of his neighbors. "Now, where did I put my keys?"

As he patted his pockets, the hair on the back of Fergus's neck stood up. There were footsteps coming his way. Grabbing his keys, he made sure his house and Jeep key were pointed outwards from his fingers, as he turned. There were no street lights in the residential block. No shifter ever needed them, and besides Fergus had been assured Arrowtown was a safe place to live.

Peering through the gloom of the night, Fergus frowned as a tall figure loitered by his letterbox. "Can I help you?" He didn't bother to raise his voice. "Are you looking for someone?"

"I was actually wondering what you were doing out so late at night. Are you just getting home?"

Fergus's shoulders relaxed. "Officer Mortimer. I know you told me you were new in town, but surely our fine Sheriff's department doesn't have you out pounding the pavements after dark? Don't you have a patrol car?"

"I like to walk." Mortimer got closer and the white of his teeth were lit up by the neighbor's porch light. "You've put in a long day, though, haven't you?" He pointed to the apron Fergus was still wearing. "I would have thought a young man like yourself would be living it up with friends at Cam's bar or driving over to Jackson to sample the nightlife over there."

Fergus chuckled, even as he shook his head. "The one thing you learn as a baker, is that the only night life you have is watching the drunks stumble home when you arrive at work at four a.m. Believe me, after seeing them, the night life holds no appeal for me."

Mortimer laughed. "Fair comment. Well, I'll let you get on with your evening, night, or whatever you want to call it. But hey, maybe you'd like to go out for a meal and a drink sometime? A quiet place, I promise and early to bed for you, you have my word."

Fergus felt his cheeks heating up. "It's nice of you to offer, Officer Mortimer, thank you. It could be a while before our schedules allow it, seeing as you've got the night shift, and I start work not long before you get off, but call in and have a muffin some time when the shop is open and we can make plans then."

"I look forward to it." Mortimer doffed his hat, and Fergus's cheeks flamed. "You take care now," he added as he walked back down the path and back into town.

Waiting until he couldn't see or hear Mortimer anymore, Fergus slapped his own hand, the one holding his keys. "Ouch, with sugar plums." Fergus shook out his sore fingers but continued telling himself off. "You, Fabulous Fergus are going to dive straight into homelessness if you're not careful. You know darn well from the gleam in his eyes that that officer wants more than a taste of your muffins, and there's no way that man is your mate. You have a business to run and your momma didn't raise you to be distracted by sexy buns in a uniform."

Fumbling his keys into the front door lock, Fergus then reached around and turned on the living room light. Stepping inside he turned to close the door when he heard it. A chesty growl coming from the huge hydrangea bush planted alongside his front path. Fergus sniffed, but he couldn't scent anyone, although he knew someone was definitely out there. "Huh, I'm more tired than I thought. Hey, Mr. Stalker in my bushes, don't go bothering me tonight, okay. My fabulous self won't be revived until I've had at least eight hours sleep. Goodnight and stay safe." He shut the door firmly, then turned the lock, because with someone outside, it was the sensible thing to do.

"Goodness, maybe I should have invited my stalker in for a meal – or better yet, get them to cook it. It would be so lovely if someone would cook for me for a change," he grumbled, reaching down to unlace his shoes. Slipping them off his swollen feet and removing his socks, Fergus padded bare foot into the kitchen. After a day around sweet things, what he craved was a bowl of delicious savory stew, and thanks to Deputy Joe's recommendations, he'd ordered half a dozen frozen meals from Mrs. Hooper. Popping a covered bowl into the microwave, Fergus wandered back through into the living room, using the remote to prime Netflix before going upstairs. "A shower, food, and sleep. It's all this Fergus needs to be Fabulous," he sang as he started taking off his clothes.

/~/~/~/~/

Is this guy for real? Hunched in his animal form, a scent blocker preventing him from being sniffed out, Cam watched as lights went on through

Fergus's house. Living room, kitchen, stairwell and finally one upstairs indicating Fergus was probably in his bedroom getting ready for a shower – an idea Cam was not going to dwell on for too long. The thought of a naked Fergus was a lot more than Cam could handle on top of his most recent revelation.

Fergus is my Fated mate. It didn't matter how much Cam wished it wasn't true, because it was, and he genuinely didn't know what to do about it. Just a whiff of Fergus's scent as he brushed past the bush Cam was hiding under was enough to make Cam want to howl – and his animal type didn't howl.

He scratched absently at the ground with his long claws and then scratched his nose. A shadow passed across the window upstairs, and Cam imagined Fergus getting ready for bed. *That's not helping,* he reminded himself crossly. *Think. Practical thoughts, damn it.* Fergus was tall, but slender and Cam found that odd because any other bull-type shifter he'd met before had been stocky. *Maybe a hybrid then?* But it's not as though Cam could tell what type just from scent and sight alone.

The looks were fine. Okay, if Cam was strictly honest with himself, Fergus looked as though he'd stepped out of Cam's dreams despite his lack of bulk. A hint of scruff around his jaw, dark eyes, and a mop of wavy black hair that framed narrow but well-defined facial features. Large rings, bangles and a black leather cuff graced his thin arms and long fingers. All fine. Cam could live with all of it. In fact, he found he quite liked the idea, but it was the man's attitude Cam couldn't understand.

The bedroom light went out, but Cam's keen ears picked up the tread of feet on stairs. Needing a closer look, he scented the air, making sure no one was near, and then padded his way to the edge of the porch, tilting his head as he did so. Fergus was singing something about waiting on a microwave. Then he heard a ding. *The microwave. Cutlery drawer. More footsteps.* Cam really wanted to look inside. Nosing his way around the porch, he carefully eased his bulk up the stairs, his ears tuned to the slightest creak.

His kind weren't known for their stealth. They were more of a lunge and eat it type of predator. But they were also incredibly smart, with long bodies and strong limbs. Cam used his body to slide up against the nearest window frame. Tilting his head around, he could see into the brightly lit living room. Fergus was sitting on a deep brown couch, eating what looked like stew from a bowl. All he had on was a pair of pink sleep pants.

Cam squinted so he could see better through the lace curtains. *Do those pants have rainbow-colored unicorns on them? Oh, my gods. They do.* If he'd been in his human form, Cam would have slapped his head and groaned. Unicorns. On a grown man. And Fergus was definitely grown. *I did not need to notice that.*

Easing his body away from the wall, Cam had enough peace of mind to use the pads of his feet as he tiptoed off the porch. Once on the grass, he scuttled around, keeping close to the base boards of the house. He needed a burrow, somewhere he could hide out until morning. He didn't think Austin would go for the midnight raid approach, but Cam learned a long time ago to cover all his bases. He'd stay in animal form, keeping a watchful eye on the house. And when Fergus had had his eight hours sleep, he'd go home, get dressed and head back. He and Fergus were going to have a serious talk, whether the young bull wanted it or not.

Chapter Five

Fergus's heart jolted when he opened his eyes and saw his room bathed in daylight. Then he remembered – Saturday. He was taking a day off. Stretching, he yawned and reached for his phone to check the time. It was just after eight. "Glorious." His grin was wide. Throwing back the covers, Fergus went through to his bathroom, doing what he had to do. He was just on his way downstairs when his phone rang.

"Momma," Fergus laughed as he answered the phone. "I haven't had my breakfast yet."

"Lay about," his momma teased. "A man like you should be ready for lunch at this time of the day."

"The shop is stocked, and I had a huge order yesterday." Making his way to the kitchen, Fergus headed for the pantry. "The Sensational Sarah is taking care of things for me there today. How are things with you?"

Listening with half an ear, Fergus collected the makings of a large pot of oatmeal. He was stirring his mixture, making sure it didn't catch on the bottom of the pan, when something his momma said made him take notice. "What do you mean Uncle Mervin's retired? He's barely forty."

"It's the way things are at home." Momma's sigh came over the phone. "He who shall not be named has been getting more territorial about the fold with every passing day. He's got some silly notion in his head that our lands are being encroached on, which is not true at all. But he insisted Mervin was needed for fold security and made the man give up his job."

"But what about Aunt Josie? You told me two weeks ago

she's just had twins." Fergus took the pot off the stove. "What will they live on without Uncle's job?"

"I don't know, sweet boy, but things will always work out. You know they will."

"Momma." Fergus could feel his anger rising and he quickly squashed it down. Anger wasn't helpful in most cases and especially with the one person who understood him. "I'm sorry. You're right. Things will always work out. Can I help, or...?"

"It's still 'or' I'm afraid my dear. Even sending money is just too risky, I'm sorry."

His momma sounded sad, and Fergus felt bad for making her feel that way. "The offer is there any time, you know that. So," he said in a deliberately bright tone. "I've been thinking about introducing the lovely people of Arrowtown to

Lamingtons. What do you think?"

Just as he hoped, his momma was diverted, and although Fergus knew she was allowing herself to be, the rest of the twenty-five-minute conversation passed quickly. Fergus could feel it, the moment the call had to end. "I love you, momma. Same time next week?" He asked quickly as the last minute ticked down.

"Love you, Fabulous Fergus." The dial tone signaled the call was disconnected.

Looking down at his overly thick oatmeal, Fergus shook his head. "This'll be fine with some honey and sweet molasses," he said out loud, determined to be upbeat. "She'll call me next Saturday," even though his animal half cautioned about the certainty.

Fergus knew things in his parents' fold were bad. The only time his momma could call him was when she was doing laundry for he who would not be named. The fact that she tried to keep the conversation light let Fergus know more than anything she actually said. The fold conditions were likely a lot worse than what his momma described. Their decision to stay... nope. Fergus wasn't going to think about it. They made their decisions and he'd made his. It was a good day. He'd heard his sweet momma's voice; the sun was shining, and, in a few moments, he'd have a full belly. Life, in that moment couldn't get any better.

He was just licking the last of his honey from his spoon, when he heard a knock at the front door. "Just a minute," Fergus called out, getting up from the kitchen table to place his bowl and spoon in the sink. Walking quickly through the living room, he peered through the nets on the side of the door. "Officer Mortimer, what are you doing here?"

Fiddling with the lock, he got the door open. Mortimer immediately stepped inside. He was still in uniform, holding his hat in his hands, and his face was deadly serious. "I'm sorry to disturb your morning, but I need to ask you to come with me, right now. My vehicle is parked just down the block."

Fergus took a step back, acutely aware he was still in his pink unicorn sleep pants. "Now? What on earth for?" He couldn't think of a thing he might have done to warrant a police visit. "How come you're still on duty. You told me you were doing the night shift. Shouldn't you be in bed getting some well-earned sleep?"

"I told Rocky I'd take care of this matter personally." The muscle under Mortimer's jaw twitched. "Come along quietly and I won't need to upset your neighbors by using the cuffs."

"Cuffs?" Folding his arms over his chest, Fergus gave the man his best glare. "You're arresting me? What for? I haven't done anything, and you know it, or you'd be able to scent I was lying, and you can't, can you."

The muscles on both sides of Mortimer's jaw were twitching now. "I just need you to accompany me..."

"Oh no." Fergus's bull could smell bullshit a mile away. "I'm not setting foot outside of this house until you tell me what's going on. Just last night you were loitering outside my house and asking me out on a date, and this morning you're trying to arrest me?" He inhaled sharply. "Was it you hiding in my bushes when I went inside? Are you my stalker?"

A furrow deepened between Mortimer's eyes. "I've never

stalked anyone in my life. Was someone in your bushes?"

Fergus waved off the question. "Probably a cat. But you don't get to divert me, Officer. I understand you have a job to do, but by my reckoning your shift finished two hours ago, so you've got no reason to be standing on my doorstep. I'll just go and give Mal a call, shall I? Maybe he'll tell me what's going on?"

"I think I'd like to know the answer to that too."

Oh, my gods, I know that voice. Fergus's eyes widened as he took in the muscled god who'd appeared behind Officer Mortimer. The chiseled face had a glimmer of a smile as the man pushed past the dumbstruck officer and held out his hand. "How do you do? My name is Cam. I believe we have some things to talk about."

"Oh Cam." Fergus took the hand offered and held on. His nose was filled with the scent of the desert – hot sand, tumbleweed and brush. "I should've known just from hearing your voice."

"Look, Cam isn't it?" Mortimer rudely interrupted the moment. "I know you work at the bar in town, but I'm here to speak to Fergus on a very important government matter. I insist you leave."

Cam took his hand back, and it was like his whole persona changed as he bumped his substantial chest against the officer's, making him back up towards the door. Mortimer suddenly looked nervous. "Listen here, Mortimer. Yes, I know who you are. I also know you're new here, so I'm going to give you some advice. We don't have 'government matters' in this town. Those orders you think you were given this morning aren't worth the paper they're printed on. I know, because I've already called Rocky and Mal and they know nothing about them, which means they didn't come through the office."

"I got the orders last night. Mal and Rocky had gone home." Mortimer eyed the street.

"Then why didn't you say something last night?" Fergus wasn't sure to make of the standoff. "Chocolate chips and sugar snaps, man, you asked me out on a date. An offer I won't be taking," he added quickly as Cam growled – the same growl Fergus remembered hearing the night before. The heat in his heart blossomed. *My mate was looking out for me. The only question is why.*

"I think I'd like to know that too," Cam said sharply. "You didn't mention that the orders didn't come through the office, you just stated two clear facts – you got orders, Mal and Rocky had already gone home. Where did those orders come from, Mortimer?"

Every word in the question was punctuated with Cam poking Mortimer's chest. The officer was now on the porch and Fergus wanted to just slam the door and hit the reset button on his day. But it was his mate facing the officer, and besides, Fergus never slammed a door. It damaged the paint work and hinges which was destructive.

The question about the orders seemed to give Mortimer his spirit back. "I don't answer to you, or Rocky and Mal. I work for someone far higher than them," he said with a snarl. Fergus shook his head. The snarl twisted the officer's features in a most unpleasant manner.

"You think you do." Cam's cryptic response had Fergus

tilting his head. "I've got a message for your boss. Do you need me to write it down?"

Mortimer shook his head.

"Tell Austin I found Mr. Ferdinand without his help. Neither one of us will be needing his services, or be following his orders, requests or anything else he feels the urge to send again. Understood? And furthermore, you can tell Austin, that if he ever dares to send his minions into this shifter town again, he won't have to worry about Ra, or Rocky and Mal, or anyone else who lives here. He'll be dealing with me personally, Camden Stone. Got it?"

Mortimer's eyes widened and his face paled. "You're Camden Stone? I had no idea." He swallowed hard. "I'll tell him. I'll call him right away."

"You do that," Cam snarled, and Fergus's heart rate skipped a beat. "And when you've done that, I suggest you march your ass down to the sheriff's office and slap your resignation on Mal's desk. I don't want to see your sorry ass around town again or I'll come after it. Deal?"

"Deal. Deal." Mortimer backed up to the steps. "I'll tell him. I'm sorry. I'll... I'll..."

"Be gone by lunchtime." Cam gave the man a final push, sending him flying down the stairs. "And for the record, I don't work in the bar, I damn well own it. Now piss off."

Scrambling to his feet, Mortimer took off running. Fergus stood in the doorway, watching the man disappear. Then he glanced over at Cam who was still bristling, *in such a hunky fashion*. "Do you think we should have that talk now, Cam, or am I supposed to call you Mr. Stone?"

Chapter Six

Nothing in Cam's morning had gone right. First, he'd overslept, dreaming sexy scenes involving his mate. He'd woken up in his human form, stark naked with the burrow he'd made the night before doing nothing to hide him from prying eyes. Slinking past waking households to get to his own place, did just as little for his piece of mind. Nudity was a shifter fact of life, but Fergus lived in a family neighborhood and there were some things little ones didn't need to see.

It took him an age to get rid of the scent blocking potion from out of his skin. He'd debated even washing it off, but continuing to wear it would have been deceitful, and Fergus deserved to know what they were to each other when they met in person. So, he scrubbed until his skin was raw which seemed to take forever.

And then, for some reason he couldn't decide what to wear. Him, who'd never cared what other people thought of him before, had a wardrobe crisis.

So, it was a lot later than Cam intended when he wandered back to Fergus's. Seeing Officer Mortimer already there stoked every jealous fire in his belly, but keen ears then stoked a fire of a different sort. Suddenly the pieces fell into place. Austin didn't have to send a man to Arrowtown. He already had one in residence. Knocking on Fergus's door before he'd had a chance to put on something more than his unicorn pants.

Cam already had Mal on speed dial before Fergus suggested it. Mal's growl and Rocky's roar told him what he already knew. Mortimer was not on official business. But using his position, trying to get Fergus to come along – fuck, it burned

Cam to the core that his mate might have disappeared without a trace, and no one would have been any the wiser except him.

And now he was here, in front of the forever promised to him by the Fates, with the knowledge Fergus's abduction would have been his fault sitting heavy in his guts. "I would love nothing more than to share your company, sit with you, eat with you and tell you anything you'd like to know. But I'm afraid our personal talk might have to wait," he said as a cruiser pulled up and an angry Rocky jumped out before the car had even stopped. Mal followed along, a little slower because he was driving, but they were both on the porch in seconds. "I need to explain a few things to Rocky and Mal as well. Mortimer was here under false pretenses, and unfortunately, it was partly my fault."

"I hope you've got coffee," Mal said crossly. "Rocky does not function well without at least three cups of the strong stuff and I could do with one myself."

"Well, isn't this a day for unusual occurrences," Fergus said brightly, swirling around and strutting into his house. Cam eyed Mal and Rocky. None of them were sure if they should follow. It wasn't until Fergus yelled, "I've got the coffee on," that the three men made their way through the house.

Fergus had made himself a comfortable home. While it was clear he hadn't been living there long, as shown by the bare walls and lack of pictures around, the furniture was comfortable, the place was sparkling clean, and the daisies sitting in a small jar on the kitchen counter reflected the warmth of the owner's personality. Cam felt immediately comfortable. It helped that Fergus's scent was the only one he could smell as they walked through.

"Fergus," Rocky groaned when he saw the plate of eclairs and muffins sitting on the white kitchen table cloth. "I swear, you know exactly the way to a man's heart. I could love you forever for just one of these muffins."

"I think Cam might have something to say about that," Mal said tartly, but his smile for Fergus was warm. "I'm sorry to intrude on your day off. I don't know what Mortimer was up to this morning, but he's clearly not loyal to Arrowtown."

"I was surprised to see him too," Fergus said. Cam found himself ushered into a chair, and a cup of coffee was placed in front of him. His fingers itched, longing to pull off his shirt and cover Fergus with it.

Bare chests and delicious eclairs were enough to tip a man like Rocky over the edge, declaring intentions Cam had no intention of letting him make.

Fergus got plates for Rocky and Mal, and Cam looked up as Fergus hovered, holding a third one. "Sensational Sarah said you don't like sweet things. Can you wait while I put some sausage rolls on or something? Maybe some small meat pies?"

"I was extremely rude to your Sensational Sarah and said things I shouldn't have done. I will apologize." Cam almost snatched the plate from Fergus's hand. "I adore sweet things and have been craving your baking since I smelled them."

Fergus just shrugged, but Cam noticed he took the chair closest to Cam, cradling a cup of sweet tea in his hand. "Okay, so does someone want to tell me what this is all about? Rocky, Mal, I promise you, I've done nothing wrong. I eat, sleep and work and that's all I've done since I arrived here. No one but my momma knows I am living here, and she would never tell a living soul. I don't understand why Mortimer was lurking by my house last night, or why he tried to arrest me this morning."

"It would seem our good friend Cam knows more about the why of what Mortimer was doing," Mal said quietly. "But you have my word, there are no warrants out for your arrest for anything. I'm only sorry, damn no, that is too soft a word. I am fucking angry that someone would abuse their uniform after all the work Rocky and I do to make sure the Sheriff's office is above reproach. It ticks me off big time, what Mortimer's done."

"He said he was working for someone bigger than the Sheriff's office." Cam physically jolted when he felt Fergus look at him directly. "And you seemed to know who that person was. Mortimer had definitely heard about you."

This was the moment Cam had been dreading. Ever since he'd left the military, he'd focused solely on making sure he was known only as a slightly grumpy bar owner who provided a safe place for his customers. "I do know who Mortimer is working for, or at least I guessed when I heard what he was saying this morning. There's a lot I can't say because of the Official Secrets Act, but I can tell you that a lot of military shifters were often lent out to other agencies for highly classified missions. I was one of them."

Cam inhaled and then let the breath out slowly.

"Unfortunately, there are some organizations that don't believe you can ever quit, and while I haven't gone out on a mission since I arrived in Arrowtown, and I am honorably discharged from the military, that doesn't stop some people from getting in touch with me infrequently, trying to tempt me to go back."

"This Austin you mentioned is one of those people, I guess?" Fergus asked.

Nodding, Cam explained, "He got in touch just this last week. Offered me an obscene amount of money for what he called a private job. But then..." Cam turned to Fergus and swallowed hard. "Austin wouldn't have even known of your existence if it hadn't been for my running searches on your background information. Austin must have set up alerts for anything I was doing, and I was searching your name, so he thought he'd talk to you. I am truly sorry."

"You were searching for information about me?" The curiosity on Fergus's face was genuine. He didn't seem angry – just confused.

"I couldn't stop thinking about you after hearing your voice," Cam confessed, wishing he didn't have Rocky and Mal for an audience. "I don't think about anyone. I have friends, lots of friends in town, but no one intimately close. I guess, I don't know. I got angry because I couldn't stop wondering what you were like, and yet..."

"You've seen so much darkness in your life," Fergus interrupted him calmly. "It's only natural to be cynical about me too. Anyone can take on the moniker 'fabulous', but very few can truly own it."

Cam didn't know whether to laugh or cry. Fortunately, Mal

spoke up, meaning he didn't have to do either. "I'm not happy that a government man was on our payroll. I'm equally not happy that this same man tried to use his position to lure an innocent like Fergus to goodness knows where for goodness knows what."

"You did a standard background check on him, I assume?" Cam asked.

"He was recommended to us by the shifter council," Mal said. "Honestly, Rocky, did you need to eat all the eclairs? I wanted one of those."

"They are soooo good," Rocky moaned around his mouthful. He choked, coughed, and then swallowed noisily. "Seriously, we need to put in a standing order for our place. I mean, Brutus is good, don't get me wrong. What he does with a chicken wing defies description. But he rarely does sweet stuff.

Are you saying we didn't check this guy out?"

Cam had to give his friend credit. Rocky came across as a bumbling fool a lot of the time, but he didn't miss much. "You'd have assumed that the council had already done all the checks you needed. There's a good chance Austin, who's a shifter too, has minions of his in every shifter town. He couldn't get a leg in here when the Quincy's were in charge, but if you sent a notice out looking for new deputies, I'd have said Austin saw an opportunity and took it."

"So, Mortimer's being here was a coincidence." Mal snatched the last éclair from Rocky's plate. "Austin's desire to chat to our new friend Fergus was because you Cam, have a suspicious nature."

"Yes." And no, that didn't make Cam feel any better especially when Fergus didn't seem to be upset at all. He just got up, grabbed the empty plate off the table and went over to a cupboard and pulled out a tin. Cam sniffed and his stomach rumbled. *Honey muffins.* He eyed Rocky who was watching Fergus's movements, his eyes gleaming.

"Is Austin the pushy type?" Fergus asked, bringing back the plate and offering it to Cam first. Cam couldn't help it. He smirked at Rocky as he grabbed three fresh muffins and put them on his plate.

"Austin doesn't understand the meaning of the word no," Cam continued after Fergus had sat down. "I'd like to think the message I gave Mortimer when I ordered him out of town would be enough, but I can't be sure."

"Are you sure this Austin fellow didn't see you as his plant in this town, seeing as he ignored your resignation from the service, and keeps pestering you to work for him?" Rocky asked, his tone suggesting he didn't appreciate not getting first pick of the muffins.

"Austin didn't know I was here." Cam bit the inside of his gum to stop from moaning out loud. He'd hit the jackpot of mates if everything Fergus created tasted as mouthwateringly delicious as his muffins.

"Well, he does now." Mal looked at Rocky who was stuffing two muffins in his mouth at the same time, while Fergus seemed to be enjoying the show. "We'd better go, before Rocky here eats poor Fergus out of house and home. Fergus, if you see anything suspicious, or you're worried about anything at all, I'll give you my number…"

"I'll be with him," Cam said quickly. "Fergus is my *mate*. At least now I understand why I was so fascinated by a man I hadn't met yet."

"Yes, well," Mal smirked. "I'd say congratulations, but your cynical nature has brought Fergus to the attention of some shadow government agency that wants to use your skills for evil and could use Fergus as leverage for that. Not to mention, you've got a lot of explaining to do to Fergus before any claiming goes on. Don't go to easy on him, Fergus. Make him work for it."

Cam had never been so happy to see the back of his friends when they left. He was nervous enough about the mating side of things, and combined with his anxiety over Austin, he thought he did well to keep his growls to himself when Fergus walked with Rocky and Mal to the front door.

Chapter Seven

Maybe I should have gone to the shop after all. Fergus leaned on his closed front door, taking a moment for himself. *No. You're being uncharitable. Cam's actions were simply… they were…* Actually, Fergus was flummoxed by Cam's actions. The man had been searching for information on him. Calling government agencies about him. Fergus had never heard about anyone being so cynical before. Especially, when at that point, he and Cam hadn't even met.

Hadn't Cam ever heard about the art of conversation? Meeting someone, talking to them, instead of investigating them? Fergus sighed. *It must be so hard living with all that cynicism all the time.* But for all his worries, Fergus's heart went out to a man who'd spent so much of his life seeing the worst type of people life could offer to the point he couldn't recognize a decent person when they were standing right in front of him. *At last I know why the Fates thought he was a good match for me.*

And because Fergus was Cam's perfect match, and he did believe in the art of conversation, he was going to have to talk to the man. Something he wasn't about to do while leaning on a door. Straightening his back, Fergus fixed on a smile and sauntered back into the kitchen. Cam was stuffing the last of his honey muffins into his mouth and that made Fergus smile wider.

"These are really good," Cam covered his mouth when he coughed. "I didn't have breakfast..."

"And you spent the night stalking my house." Fergus went over to his stove top, pulling a pan off the hook above it. "I had oatmeal for breakfast, but I'm happy to whip you up some bacon and eggs, while you talk to me." Without waiting for Cam's reply, he got the items he needed and turned on the stove. Within seconds the smell of cooking bacon filled the air.

"Talking is not one of my strong points."

Fergus stayed focused on the pan. He knew sometimes it was easier to talk to someone when they weren't being stared at.

"I find it difficult to let people get close to me – beyond friends, I mean."

"I imagine, if you've seen a lot of bad things in your life, trusting people would be hard to do." Fergus pushed the bacon to one side with his spatula and cracked four eggs into the pan. "I've never heard a bad word said about you in this town though. Not that I've been here very long. From all accounts, you really care about the people here, you're considered a great catch and half the single population drool over you, from a respectful distance of course."

"I never encourage that sort of thing, the drooling I mean."

Fergus was pleased Cam didn't discount how popular he was. False modesty was never a good look and claiming he didn't notice how attractive he was to others would indicate Cam lived with blinkers on.

"I never wanted the bad stuff I've been through to touch the innocent lives of people who live here."

There was a wealth of connotation in that statement. Noting the eggs were cooked, Fergus found a plate and flipped the bacon and eggs onto it, before searching for a knife and fork. "Here," he said, putting the plate in front of his mate when he'd found the cutlery. "It's not much, but it will hold you over until lunch."

Cam moved fast. Fergus's hand was caught before he had a chance to move. "I can totally understand why you claim the moniker 'Fabulous'" he said gravely, as Fergus met his eyes. "No one has ever done anything like this for me before."

"It'll cost you." Fergus showed his teeth indicating his tease. "I fully expect to be adored by my mate. Accepting anything less would be an insult to my wonderful nature. Failure to provide that adoration will result in cooked goods being withheld until any issues are fully rectified to my satisfaction."

"Ooh, I can see you're going to be the one wearing the pants in this relationship." Cam leaned over his plate, inhaling deeply. "Hmm. Withholding good food like this seems like harsh punishment. I'd better be on my best behavior."

"Eat up before it gets cold." Fergus let his fingers linger as he withdrew his hand from Cam's grasp. While his mate ate, Fergus occupied himself with making more coffee and a cup of tea for himself. He was happy enough to watch Cam eat – fast, economical movements Fergus imagined his mate learned in the military. Cam didn't let one morsel of food go to waste, and when he finally scraped his plate clean, before leaning back and patting his belly with a satisfied sigh, Fergus felt a warm blast of appreciation run right through him.

"We do need to talk," Cam said ruefully. "Before any claiming takes place, you need to know what you're getting into."

A quick shaft of guilt pierced Fergus's spirit. There were some things Cam was going to have to know about him too before any claim was made. Studying his mate, Fergus could see Cam was tired. "You slept outside last night, didn't you?" He asked softly, reaching out and resting his hand on Cam's. "You knew this Austin fella was looking for me before Mortimer showed up?"

Cam nodded. "Austin called me last night. Thanks to my efforts, he had a file on you, gleaned from his own sources I imagine. He got curious, never a good thing for a rhino to be, and decided he needed to talk to you to find out why I was so interested in what you were doing. That scared me, and I've not been scared of much in my life."

"A rhino?" Fergus scratched his head. "They aren't known for listening to others. Why would he want to talk to me?"

"He was determined I'd do this job for him and that doesn't

make sense either. Austin has dozens of covert operatives he can call in, even for a private job. The money he offered this time was obscene, and then he threatened to take you. That's not the way things are usually done."

Not knowing the major players, Fergus didn't know what was considered normal in a covert situation. "You wanted to protect me, which means your instincts are in the right place. Have you ever thought about finding out more about this Austin fellow, and why he's being so insistent this time about you doing this specific job?"

"Investigating him comes with its own risks." Cam sighed and Fergus longed to give the man a great big hug. "But then, in the past, I've always worried Austin would find out where I live. With Mortimer's big mouth, Austin will already know that now."

"Will we have to leave Arrowtown?" Fergus's heart dropped at the thought. He'd put in so much work in his new bakery and he'd finally found a house he really loved.

But Cam shook his head. "I'm not letting him, or the fear of what he might do, drive us out of our home. Among Austin's circles my name is feared, and for good reason. I've made a lot of friends in this town who'd support us if it becomes necessary. With luck, now that Austin knows where I am, he'll just leave us alone."

Yeah, and the tooth fairy dresses in black and drives a hearse in their spare time. But Fergus didn't say that. Instead, he ran his fingers up Cam's massive bicep, and said softly, "You need to rest. I imagine you've also got a bar to open in just a few hours. Come with me. I want to show you why I bought this particular house."

To his credit, Cam didn't demur, didn't object, he just stood up when Fergus did, and picked up his plate, popping it into the sink before following Fergus through into his wet room. "I adore gardens, but I hate gardening," Fergus explained as he unlocked the back door. "Apparently, the horse shifter who had this house before me, put in a lot of gardens, but the house was empty for some time before I bought it, and they got a bit out of hand. But I love it, just the way it is. See?"

/~/~/~/~/

Fuck, this is a security nightmare, was Cam's initial thoughts at seeing the overgrown yard. All plot sizes were big in Arrowtown, and Fergus's yard stretched at least fifty yards from the back door – that he could see. The boundary itself was obscured with big over grown trees and bushes, totally obliterating any sign of the neighbors. Closer toward the house were raised gardens, also overflowing with a mixture of flowers, herbs and vegetables.

"A lot of this is self-seeding," Fergus said excitedly as they stepped outside. "The plants have learned to co-exist with each other. There was a heap of dead plants I had to pull out when I first arrived but look at it now."

"It's lovely." Cam managed the compliment automatically, but his brain was already mentally measuring the grass distance between the house and bushes. *This is good, this is all right,* he thought, taking in the thin branches on the tall trees that would be useless at supporting a sniper. The wide swathe of grass area would make creeping up on the house highly difficult, and the thickness of the bushes and undergrowth would mean anyone coming through that way would be heard before they were seen.

"This is one of my favorite spots," Fergus said, catching his hand and dragging him along. He flung himself down on some moss that was growing at the base of a huge tree. Slower, and with a lot more caution, Cam did the same. "Lie back," Fergus urged. "Tell me what you see. Isn't it beautiful?"

Repressing a sigh, because Cam was not one of those men who liked to imagine shapes in the clouds or anything like that, he did note that the moss was thick and cool under his back, thanks to the shade. Looking up, Cam found himself staring at an intricate canopy – thin branches covered in a mass of leaves, all spreading out from each other creating a lacework of black and green against the bright blue sky.

"We had a tree like this at home," Fergus whispered. "Back before, well, before things changed, me and my momma used to lie under it every chance we got, dreaming of all the places we wanted to visit. It was like, if you concentrated on the leaves and sky, you could be anywhere in the world in that moment. I still feel the same way."

"You were close to your momma?"

"I still am," Fergus let out a long breath. "Or at least I am as close to her as I can be right now. I spoke to her on the phone today. That is always a great way to start the day."

Cam's spidey senses immediately activated. But the air was warm, the moss was cool, and the gentle movements of the leaves were soothing. "I never take the time to do this," he said softly, preserving the confessional mood. "It's amazing how much you miss, when you're busy all the time."

"You know what's even better?" There was a rustle of clothing as Fergus moved. Seconds later, Fergus was draped across Cam's chest, his arms splayed around his torso in a hug. "Cuddling is always good for what ails you," Fergus said, his head resting on the middle of Cam's chest. "Especially, when you've had a rough night."

You smell amazing, Cam thought as he slowly closed his eyes.

Chapter Eight

Fergus woke up alone. He wasn't surprised. A teeny tiny bit hurt, but not enough to make a fuss about it. From the position of the sky overhead, it had to be about lunchtime, and Fergus's stomach grumbled, letting him know oatmeal could only stem his hunger for so long. His thoughts immediately went to Cam, who had probably gone to open his business. *I could go and see him,* Fergus mused, watching the play of shadows from the leaves above dance on his chest. *I could take him a meal seeing as his cook left yesterday. Or I could do laundry. Hmm. Decisions. Decisions.*

He chuckled. As if there was really any choice in the matter. Fergus had a mountain of clothes and only one Cam, and it's not as though he'd ever been to the bar before. "But what to make him," he muttered to himself, as he sauntered back to the house. He frowned as he noticed a shadow passing across his window. Too small to be Cam, but whoever it was shouldn't have been in his house.

Sprinting, because damn it, his home was his castle, Fergus powered through the wet room door, through the kitchen and into the living room, his arm raised, and his fist clenched. There was a high-pitched scream, and someone cowered on the floor. "The door was open; it was open I swear."

"Sarah? My darling wee Sarah, I'm so sorry I scared you." Fergus dropped to his knees and cuddled the frightened girl. "What were you doing creeping around my house, sweet one? Why didn't you call out to me?"

"The door was open," Sarah sobbed. "I brought the till money round, and the door was open, and I thought maybe a burglar was in here and..."

"And you dashed in to save me." Fergus gave Sarah a huge hug. "That was so brave of you and very silly too, you realize that, don't you?"

"I was scared I'd find the best boss in the world dead on the floor."

Fergus held the frightened rabbit close as she sobbed. Young adult drama aside, the open front door was a real concern. There was no way Cam would have left it that way and he distinctly remembered closing it when Mal and Rocky left. Which meant someone else, not Sarah, had been in his house and might even still be around.

"Sweetness, sweetness," he repeated as Sarah hiccupped. "Listen to me. Listen. Are you listening?" Tilting Sarah's head back carefully, he waited until she nodded. "I need you to go to the bar for me, okay? I need you to run as fast as you can and go and tell Cam what you found here."

Sarah blinked twice. "Can't you phone him?"

I need you to be in a place of safety, you clueless bundle of sweetness. "I don't have his number, sweet thing, but look, Cam's my mate, and I need to stay here and make sure nothing's been stolen, so if you can..."

"Oh, my god, oh, my god, I knew it, I just knew it, I could feel it in my fur." Fergus almost choked as thin arms strangled his neck. "You will be just perfect for him and he couldn't have gotten a more fabulous mate. I'm so happy for you both!"

"Yes, yes, well, we still have a number of things to work out, but look can you...?"

"I'll go. I'll go." Sarah jumped to her feet. "I won't stop and talk to anyone. I'll run straight to the bar and I'll make sure Cam's the only one I tell about this. Oh, my god, Fergus, your own mate, that's so exciting."

Fergus flashed his teeth, because honestly Sarah's excitement was contagious, but his smile slipped the moment she sprinted out of the still open door. He just knew someone as paranoid and cynical as Cam would not have left his front door wide open. *And I definitely closed it.* The only question was if the intruder was still on the premises.

Pushing himself to his feet, Fergus called on his animal side. He didn't have the best of noses, but any shifter could sniff out strange scents especially in their home. His bull was cautious, but curious for now, which was probably a good thing. Shifting in his house was not an option. *Front door step first,* he decided, but as he stepped towards it, a plank of wood on the flooring upstairs creaked. *Sugar plum cookies and fairy dust. I'm going to need a weapon.*

/~/~/~/~/

I wonder if he's woken up yet. Cam was resting his elbow on the bar, staring out at nothing, thinking about his mate. He hadn't wanted to leave Fergus. The young man made such a fetching picture, his innocence shining through even as he slept and the way he relaxed so trustingly in Cam's arms, set his hormones and protective instincts into overdrive.

But the bar needed to be opened. Regulars like Dave Hooper and his cronies kicked up a hell of a fuss if the doors to his place were open just one second late. Darwin took the weekends off, and Nicky and

Sue wouldn't be arriving until four pm. Which meant Cam not only had to open, but he had to run the bar himself for five hours before he could even think about leaving to see Fergus again.

"What are we going to do for grub now Mary's got herself knocked up?" Dave Hooper slammed his empty jug on the counter which was his polite way of saying he wanted a refill. "You're supposed to serve food with booze you know, otherwise some of these young buggers will get silly."

"Has your niece put you on a diet as well as a budget?" Cam grinned as he reached for a fresh jug and filled it.

"She keeps thinking she knows what's best for me." Dave patted his ample middle. "There's nothing wrong with the way I'm built."

Cam wisely left that statement alone, pushing the now-filled jug in Dave's direction. "Mary never used to do lunches over the weekend, so I don't know why you're griping today."

"I'm thinking about Monday, aren't I?" Dave tapped his skull. "Forward planning. I need to know if I have to ask that niece of mine for a packed lunch."

"I'll arrange something," Cam promised. "I was thinking about asking Fergus from the bakery to supply some of his goods until I can get another cook seeing as Hazel is so busy at the diner."

"You mean supply sandwiches and shit?" Dave almost spit out the mouthful of beer he'd taken. "What are you trying to do to me? Oh wait. Wait a minute. Is that Fergus the young one who baked all those goods we had yesterday?"

"I saw more than sandwiches on those platters," Cam nodded.

"Hmm. That could be all right." Dave stuck his nose in the air. "So long as he doesn't bring in any healthy shit, he'll do fine."

Cam chuckled as Dave ambled over to three of his cronies who seemed to spend all their waking hours in his bar. He had no idea what they had to talk about, spending so much time together as they did, but heaven help any of them if they missed a day. Mind you, all four men were sharp minded and had keen ears. There wasn't anything that went on in town they didn't know about.

The bar wasn't busy, but for a Saturday afternoon that wasn't unusual. Family units spent time working on their houses and doing gardening chores, or they took the drive over to Jackson to shop. Kids played sports, and that always kept parents busy. Cam knew his business wouldn't pick up until later when the dedicated drinkers had had enough of family time for one day. For now, he noticed Roger, the slick rabbit who thought Cam didn't know about his pool hustling was playing at the table with a couple of friends. For once Roger had dressed down for the day, not playing to his obvious attributes like he normally did. *I wonder if he's scented his mate,* Cam thought as he checked that the fridges were stocked.

The other three drinkers weren't local, but Cam had met them before, so he wasn't worried about them. The wolf shifters ran a trucking company, and often popped in on their way through to the larger towns. It'd been on the tip of his tongue to say to any of them, that if they were mate hunting then they'd do better in an afternoon wandering Arrowtown's streets. But Cam didn't get involved in his patrons' affairs unless they asked him to.

I wonder if Fergus would bring me lunch. The muffins and breakfast were a distant memory. Part of Cam's animal attributes was that he ate, a lot. When his bar door opened, Cam's head shot up, along with his hopes, but it wasn't Fergus, it was Sarah. The young rabbit was flushed as though she'd been running, and he immediately checked to see if anyone was following her, but there was no one else.

Sliding to a stop halfway to the bar, Sarah bent over, her hands on her knees as she tried to catch her breath. "Cam. Thank the gods," She puffed. She straightened up, resting her hand on her heaving chest. "I've seriously got to stop eating Fergus's cooking. Honestly."

"Is something wrong with Fergus?" Cam leaped over the

bar counter and hurried to her side. But one of the wolf shifters got there first.

"Who's Fergus?" The wolf shifter growled, as he leaned over, sniffing deliberately at Sarah's neck. He had to be a foot taller than the much smaller rabbit.

"Seriously?" Sarah tilted her delicate nose in the wolf's direction. "Huh. Unexpected. Okay. But you have to wait a minute. Fergus is this man's mate and I think he's in trouble."

"What happened to Fergus? He was sleeping when I left." Cam grabbed Sarah's shoulders, and twisted her around, causing the wolf to growl more. "For fuck's sake, shut up, wolfy. She's yours, you're hers, whoopie, but I want to hear about Fergus."

"The door." Sarah's gaze went back and forth between the wolf and Cam, finally resting on

Cam. "Did you leave Fergus's front door wide open, only I went there, to take his money you see, and the door was open, but Fergus was out the back. And then he came running in because he must have seen me, but he'd only just woken up, and he told me to run here..."

"Fucking hell." Cam's eyes darted around his customers. Dave would drink his taps dry; Roger would hand out free drinks to all his friends. *Fergus!* His eyes landed on the huffing wolf. "You, what's your name?"

"Pierce, but what's it to you? I just met my mate..."

"Yes, yes, yes, and you want to whisk her away and claim her in the trees or some shit, but Sarah deserves to be treated better than that. She at least deserves a meal first. So, here's what you're going to do. You are going to take this precious rabbit, you are going to stash her behind the bar and keep her safe, and she is going to serve drinks for me until I get back, okay? You should know how to use the till Sarah, it's probably the same type as Fergus uses and all the prices are marked on it."

"You can't make me..." The wolf was starting to posture, puffing out his chest and widening his shoulders.

"Please!" Sarah turned her big eyes on her new mate, and Cam would've laughed if his situation wasn't so dire. The wolf just melted, right there in front of his eyes. "Fergus is my boss, and he's the best boss in the world. He calls me Sensational Sarah and no one has ever done that before and he's Cam's mate but they haven't done the deed yet, and he could be in trouble, and I just couldn't give you all my attention if I'm worried about him because that's just how I am. Please, you can keep me safe here, can't you?"

Yep, that wolf is a gonna, Cam thought as Pierce stood up straighter, and offered Sarah his arm. "Go," Pierce said, "I'll take care of Sensational Sarah and the bar. Run."

Cam ran. Yes, he could have taken his jeep, but there was no point when Arrowtown was such a small place. His house was only two blocks away from the bar, and Fergus's house was only two blocks further out from that. The streets were quiet, only a few families out in their gardens who waved as he ran past. Cam barely noticed; his attention fixed on Fergus's house. He was almost at the garden path, when he heard the sound of breaking glass, and Fergus came flying out of an upstairs window.

"Oh, my gods, Fergus!" His heart in his mouth, Cam ran to his mate's body that was sprawled across the lawn. Fergus's chest was still moving, although there were bruises on his face and a trickle of blood leaking across one closed eye. As Cam leaned down, Fergus's eyes fluttered and then opened and Fergus reached up, palming his own head.

"Well, flutter-butts," he said wincing as more blood appeared on his hands. "That didn't go the way I had hoped and anticipated." He looked around, before his eyes landed on Cam. "They got my rolling pin."

Chapter Nine

Fergus was the first to admit his Fabulousness came with limitations. He could keep his jeep serviced and running smoothly with no problems at all. Clean out a blocked drain – child's play. Slap a three-tiered wedding cake in front of him and tell him to ice roses on it in under ten minutes and he could do it. Dancing, music, anything artistic and Fergus would give it a go and not make a fool of himself.

Fighting, however, was one of his limitations. Honestly, as he'd silently crept up his stairs to confront an intruder, when all his senses were telling him he should have run with Sarah, Fergus was blaming his animal spirit. His Highland bull was just too big for him to shift inside. *I wouldn't even get my shoulders up this staircase in my furry self, let alone my horns* he'd thought at the time, clutching a rolling pin in one hand. It was all he had. *Maybe I've been invaded by mice shifters, or squirrels, or something equally small and cute.*

But the mean faces of the two intruders who were going through his dresser draws annihilated that hope. And the scent. Fergus wanted to sneeze. There was nothing skankier than a couple of jackals who didn't know how to use a shower.

"What are you doing in my house? Get out of my things!" Fergus had done his best to look as intimidating as possible, not easy to do when his hair kept flopping in a lovely wave across half his face. He tightened the grip on his rolling pin. "You've got no right to be in here. I demand you leave immediately."

The two men straightened. *At least they hadn't gotten to my bottom drawer yet,* Fergus thought with relief. He did not want his fancy lace corsets, delicate silky underwear, and his small but perfectly adequate toy collection being pawed over by smelly brutes.

"*You're* the bull shifter?" One jackal sneered elbowing his friend. "I thought you was going to be a huge muscled dude or something."

"I can assure you, I'm perfectly big enough to defend my home," Fergus said staunchly. He waved his rolling pin in what he hoped was a threatening manner. "Get out. Don't ever come back."

"Make us." The second jackal had the same sneer. Fergus wondered idly if the two men were brothers, but he didn't have time for thinking after that because the two men charged him. *At the same time, that's so unfair.* Swinging his rolling pin around as hard as he could, Fergus was determined to leave the men bruised if nothing else, but it seemed the jackals had rocks for brains because nothing stopped them.

Punches to the head, a kick to his stomach; Fergus didn't even have time to groan. He was making hits of his own, he knew he was, because one of the guys howled and clutched at his arm, before kicking Fergus in the chest. *Maybe Cam can teach me some self-defense moves,* he thought as he doubled over, but it was thoughts of Cam that kept him fighting.

He had only held the delicious man, who, Fergus realized would make mincemeat of two jackals and think nothing about it. But Fergus had laid down his challenge. Cam was supposed to adore him, and his mate couldn't do that if he was dead. So, he hit back, swinging his rolling pin wildly, trying to get the guys to just give him some room so he could actually hit something breakable.

But then a hand came up, his rolling pin was wrenched from his hand and before Fergus knew what was happening, his breath whooshed out after a hard shove to his chest and he heard the sound of glass breaking. He just had time to realize *I'm flying,* before he landed on his back with a thud.

The fall winded him. It took a moment for Fergus to open his eyes and he reached for his aching head automatically. "Well, flutter-butts," he said wincing as blood appeared on his hands. "That didn't go the way I had hoped and anticipated." He looked around, before his eyes landed on Cam. "I dropped my rolling pin."

"Who? Where?" Cam reminded Fergus of a human minotaur, his nostrils flaring, his eyes black and flashing with another presence Fergus couldn't identify.

"Two." Fergus held up two of his fingers, or he thought he did. His eyesight was still a bit blurry. "Jackals. In my room. My bedroom." Cam was up like a shot, racing towards the house. "Don't let them see what's in my bottom drawer," Fergus yelled as his head slumped back on the grass again. "That would be so embarrassing," he muttered. He ran his hand through his wavy hair, and grimaced. The blood was already drying so it was sticky. "I need to shift. A shower. Something to wear other than unicorn pants might be a good idea. Darn it, and I was going to make Cam lunch."

"How about you lie still, until we can make sure you've not got a serious head injury."

Fergus blinked. His eyes were watery, so he tried again. He could make out two large shapes in front of him. "Is that you, doc? Is Deputy Joe with you? Only there are two jackals..." He tried to point to the house, but the Doc was stronger than he looked, or maybe his arm had stopped working.

"Lie still, you young fool. I don't know if you've broken anything yet."

Fergus felt a slight prick in his arm, and then his head was filled with clouds. "You have such a lovely bedside manner," he whispered, or at least he thought he did. He found it difficult to speak when he was floating.

/~/~/~/~/

Cam pulled his fist back just in time as Deputy Joe came around the bedroom door. "They're fucking gone, probably out of the back door. They must have realized someone would come running with the sound of breaking glass." He was snarling, his fangs half out, but Cam didn't care. Someone had broken into his mate's lovely home, and gone through his precious things.

"I'll call Rocky," Joe pulled a phone out of his jean's pocket. "He's got the best nose for tracking, unless you wanted..."

Oh, Cam wanted all right. He wanted nothing more than to find the assholes who hurt his mate and rip out their guts and dance in their blood while their eyes were still pleading with him to stop. The throat slash that killed them would be the final act, not the first. But he had to think of Fergus – shit. Cam closed his eyes. He could still see his mate's body flying out of the window and landing with a splat on the unforgiving ground. "Call Rocky and see if Dan from the hardware store can send someone over to board up the window.

Apologize to him for me, for disturbing his Saturday."

"Fergus is going to be all right," Joe said, laying a comforting hand on Cam's shoulder, that he barely resisted shaking off. "Doc's with him and he's his normal grumbly self which means the young bull is going to be fine. I just don't understand... Were you just passing by, or..."

"I thought Mal would have told you. Fergus is my mate. Unclaimed, but you know, we only met this morning." Cam ran a hand over his head. He could still smell Fergus's blood and his animal wanted to savage something with his teeth, but he knew he had to pull himself together.

"I haven't seen Mal or Rocky today," Joe said. "Doc and I called into the bar for a quiet drink and Sarah told us what was going on. We got here as fast as we could."

"Appreciated," and Cam did appreciate it. He loved how caring everyone was in Arrowtown even if he didn't show a lot of that love himself. "I'm just going to..." He waved at the stairs.

Joe nodded. "I'm sure he'll be fine, but you see to Fergus, I'll get Rocky on the trail and organize the window clean up."

Clumping down the stairs, Cam checked the time on his phone. It was a little after two. Bringing up his contacts, he hit one of them. "Nicky? It's Cam. Can you start your shift early for me please?"

"Sure, I can be there in twenty minutes if you need me. Just let me have a quick shower. Have we got busy?"

"I don't know." Cam swallowed hard around the lump in his throat. "Sarah, the little rabbit shifter that works for Fergus is minding the bar with her new wolf mate. I'm at Fergus's, I just found out today he's my mate. He's been hurt. I don't know when I'm coming in."

There was a moment's silence, and then Nicky said, "Sure thing, boss. Leave it to me. We'll close up for you tonight if that's what it takes and if you need a few days, just let me, Sue or Darwin know, and we'll cover for you. You focus on what's important. Congratulations boss." The call went dead.

Relief. As Cam pocketed his phone and headed back out Fergus's front door, all he felt was overwhelming relief. That was one of the joys of living in a shifter town. Everyone accepted the importance of mates, everyone chipped in, helped out and did what they could for their neighbors. Oh, not all shifters were wonderful people. The Quincy family was a proven example of that, but for the most part, and in

Arrowtown in particular, everyone pitched in to help and Cam had never been so thankful he'd picked Arrowtown as his home.

Walking outside, he stopped on the porch. There, standing on the grass was a massive animal with lethal looking horns that were at least four feet across. A giant head housed big dark eyes, barely visible under the long fringe that hung from between his ears. Tufts of the lawn were hanging out of his mouth as the bull kept up a slow chewing motion. The darkness of his fur was the same shade as Fergus's hair. There was a gentle peacefulness about the animal, despite his size, and Cam felt his shoulders relax.

"I had to give him a sedative, just a short acting one so I could reset his spine," Doc said gruffly. "Damn bastards broke his lower back, but Fergus probably didn't realize it as he was all fired up with adrenalin. He shifted easily enough, and I didn't let him stand up until I knew his bones had fused right. He should be fine. There might be a few lingering symptoms of concussion when he shifts back from the numerous head injuries he had, but I'm sure you know what to look out for."

Cam nodded. He couldn't take his eyes off the gentle giant. He knew he was going to get angry. He was probably going to be downright shitty once he thought about the extent of Fergus's injuries and how easily he could have died. But for now, he just wanted to bask in the fact that Fergus was alive. "Thanks, Doc. I.., anything I can do for you..."

"Just make sure that young mate of yours keeps baking. He makes a custard cream to die for." Doc stomped off, probably to go and find his own mate in the house. Cam guessed Mrs. Hooper was watching their twins.

Fergus, as a bull, was still watching him steadily, his big mouth scrunching around the grass he was eating, only his tail and ears flicking occasionally. Moving slowly, Cam went down the steps, and across the lawn, his lips twitching in a semblance of a smile. Fergus didn't move, letting Cam walk right up to his chest.

"I'm so glad you're okay," Cam whispered, wrapping his arms loosely around the bull's thick neck. "If you had died…" He couldn't even complete the sentence. He just leaned his face on Fergus's neck and breathed slowly and evenly. He felt the heavy weight of Fergus's head resting over his shoulder, and in that moment, Cam felt true peace.

Chapter Ten

"I didn't know there were jackals in town," Fergus said, blowing on his nail polish. Cam was in the kitchen, cooking, and for some reason, the stubborn male wouldn't let him help. So, deciding he needed a pick me up, Fergus perched on one of his bar stools, his foot up and set about painting his toenails. He'd already laid a base coat of pink and was now debating whether he needed any decorations. He frowned when Cam didn't answer. "I thought jackals lived in human areas. They don't like shifter towns."

"That's because for the most part jackals are mean, selfish and lie through their eye teeth most of the time." Cam hunted through the cupboards and pulled out a grater. "And you're right, they weren't locals, so your bottom drawer secrets are safe. Rocky traced their scent out of town, so it's unlikely they're coming back."

The heat on Fergus's cheekbones was intense. "You looked in my drawer."

"The jackals were looking for something. I had to know you weren't hiding government secrets in there."

Fergus narrowed his eyes in Cam's direction. The big man was scattering grated cheese over a large casserole. "Are you smirking?"

"Nope." Cam lifted the casserole and slid it into the oven. Closing the oven door, he grabbed a dish cloth and wiped his hands. "Dinner will be ready in twenty minutes and for the record, I don't smirk. I just might have been slightly happy about your non-governmental secret stash."

"I think some things should remain private until after the claiming bites have been shared," Fergus grumbled, but secretly he was pleased with Cam's response. The big man had been so attentive, putting the money Sarah had brought over away in Fergus's safe, dealing with Rocky and Mal, and the host of nosey neighbors who all wanted to know what was going on. Fergus's window was fixed, with glass and not the plywood Cam had ordered, and at least a dozen people all patted his shoulder, while he was still in furry form, and wished him well.

All Fergus had done was stand like a lump on a log, on all four feet, quietly chewing, watching the business, not even flinching when the twins from two doors down jumped up and tried swinging on his horns. It was Cam who finally got everyone to leave, and Cam that waited patiently with a blanket while Fergus shifted back. *The damn man didn't even take a peek at my body when I shifted, but he looks in my drawers. What does that tell me about him as a person?*

Not that it mattered what type of person Cam was. Fergus was subject to the mating pull as much as any shifter would be. His bull was a placid and quiet animal, but that didn't mean he hadn't been suffering with the hard on from hell for the past hour and a half. And Cam hadn't touched him. Even when he wrapped Fergus in a blanket, he didn't touch any bare skin.

"Did you want to watch a movie or something?" It seemed Cam had tidied up while Fergus was wool-gathering and was now looking at him expectantly.

"We don't have to." Fergus hoped his grin wasn't showing his evil side. "Come, sit beside me. We've still got a lot to learn about each other and I'd far rather talk to you than drool over some stud on the television."

Cam did sit, but not beside him as Fergus hoped. Instead, he pulled one of the bar stools to the end of the kitchen counter and sat there, one eye on the oven door and one eye on Fergus.

I can work with that. "So, tell me, I don't know what type of animal you share your spirit with, and honestly, that's fine, because as you know some people are a little embarrassed about their shifted size." Cam's jaw tightened and inside Fergus giggled. "But what do you think about sex and how does that relate to your shifter side? I mean, us bulls are built as the name implies, which can cause problems if you're with a human, and I know wolf shifters have sex so often it's a wonder their dicks don't fall off. Cat shifters have that innate grace just like their furry selves, and my gods, have you ever had sex with a squirrel shifter? They just don't shut up."

A stuttered growling erupted from Cam's throat and the man's fists were clenched so tight his knuckles were white. Fergus decided to ignore all that tension and inspected his toenails. They were dry, which was handy for what he had planned next.

"Of course, not all animal halves translate into sexual behavior. I mean, take rabbits for example. Everyone jokes about 'going at it like rabbits' but rabbit shifters stay virgins until they meet their mate or bond with someone. And then you have to think about elephants, don't you? I mean, can you imagine how big an elephant shifter's cock would be." Fergus held his hands out as though imagining it. "I mean, what if he was fated mates with a mouse. Oh, my gods, that could be trouble. And snake shifters. I mean, has anyone ever seen a snake's penis. Aren't they all like tucked up in their body somehow? Oh, that's right, Darwin has seen one because of Simon, but I mean..."

"Can we talk about something else?" A sneaky side peek at Cam had Fergus wanting to howl with laughter. The man's face was red, and he had a huge vein popping out the side of his temple.

"But it's so interesting, don't you think?" Fergus would not be deterred. "I mean, we are our animals, but we're not, and you have to wonder how much influence our animal halves have over our human sex drives. Think about it. Bulls can rut until the cows come home, which is really funny because cows do come home if the bull is calling for them, and then, well, I don't know what you are, but it's not like there's an asexual animal type, is there?"

"Fergus!" There was so much grit in that one word, Fergus pictured Cam spitting out gravel.

"You have to feel sorry for all the little shifters, well, don't you?" Fergus mentally hummed a happy tune. "Think about them, with their tiny cute dicks, although maybe for them, there isn't a correlation. I mean, maybe their dick sizes are proportional to the form they take at the time – like in their fur it's teeny tiny, and then in their human form, if they're a big bloke..."

"I'm a honey badger! A, don't give a fuck, all animals fear us, honey badger!" Cam stood up so fast, his stool fell over.

Fergus wanted to bellow in triumph. His mate's jeans were so tented it's a wonder Cam could stand up straight. Looking up, Fergus flipped his hair out of his eyes and smiled sweetly. "Do they have a big dick? Only, I've never seen one."

/~/~/~/~/

Cam's jeans were so tight, they were threatening to tear. His skin was hot, his blood felt as though it was burning a trail through his veins and every time he inhaled he could smell Fergus's musky arousal. Cam had been in that state for freaking hours.

But Cam had handled it. In fact, while he'd been making a casserole, he'd been mentally patting himself on the back for not plastering Fergus's slender body over the kitchen counter and fucking into him like a man possessed. His mate had broken his back that afternoon and while Cam knew on an intellectual level, Doc wouldn't have given him the okay for sex before leaving unless he was absolutely sure Fergus was fine, there was an emotional side of Cam that couldn't stop seeing the image Fergus made as he went flying out of the window.

Fergus wanted to talk instead of watching a blissfully distracting movie, and Cam was fine with that because mates did need to learn about each other. But instead of asking him his favorite color, or about the bar, or anything considered a safe conversational topic for a first date situation, Fergus started talking about sex. Or more specifically dick size, and while Cam was sure he was being baited, he couldn't help but respond.

So, he spoke up. Cam couldn't help it. He told his deepest secret that no other living person knew. And what did Fergus do? Did he react with horror? Did he screw up his nose in disgust? No. All Fergus did was look at him with those amazing eyes and ask him if he had a big dick.

"What do you think?" He roared waving his hands in the direction of the front of his jeans where his dick size was implied even if it wasn't blatantly on show. "This isn't a sock puppet. I've been fucking horny for hours, and no, no, before you open those luscious lips of yours again, I am not fucking you because in case you'd forgotten, you broke your back today."

Fergus grinned, reaching behind himself, arching that spine Cam was so worried about and running his hands down it slowly. He tilted his head back, showing off a gorgeous long neck and made a satisfied moan. "My back feels fine to me. Maybe you should touch it and see for yourself if you're so worried."

"Fergus." Cam gripped the sides of the kitchen counter, his head bowed as he tried to control himself. "I swear, if I touch you, I won't be able to hold back. I'll have your pants off and your ass over that counter so fast..."

"Like this?" Cam heard the sound of skin slap. *Don't look. Don't look.*

Cam couldn't help himself. He looked. The loose sweats that Fergus put on after his shower were pooled around his ankles, a bright rosy red mark showing where Fergus had slapped his own butt cheek. His forearms were resting on the counter, and his torso was hunched over them, so his ass stuck out. And then he wiggled his hips – a saucy little side wiggle showing off sexy glute muscles.

"Or maybe, you had something like this in mind." Fergus

kicked off his sweats, turned and hopped up on the bench, lying back and spreading his legs.

Mother of God, help me. He's wearing a butt plug. There was only so much torture a man could take and while Cam's animal half did contribute to his nature – it was the nature of take what you want and to hell with possible consequences. Yes, the honey badger was thinking about food, but he also wanted a claimed mate. Cam's hands reached out before he knew what he was doing, pulling on Fergus's ankles until the man's butt was just over the counter top. He fisted the leaking length splayed across Fergus's belly.

"The counter is the perfect height, don't you think?" Fergus had the audacity to wink. "Good thing you're so tall."

Cam didn't bother answering. The time for talking was over. Cam gave Fergus's wide, long cock one quick glance, and then bent down, widening his lips as far as they could go, so he could get the head of it in his mouth. There was no way he could get Fergus's entire length down his throat without a hell of a lot of practice, but Cam had a strong suck and a wide hand. Fergus was writhing in seconds.

There was nothing better, in Cam's opinion, than the taste of male cock on his tongue. He didn't have it often. He was usually the one being sucked, and it was just as easy to finish a random guy off by hand when they were both in a hurry. But Fergus's groin held concentrated scent, and that, combined with the juices Cam was sucking up was pure ambrosia. He worked his hand, gently at first, but then with more firmness as he longed to taste more.

"Take it out," Fergus pleaded. Cam stopped sucking but he didn't take his mouth off his new mate's cock. "Take it out, it's teasing my prostate. I'm going to blow."

Actually, I think I'm the one giving the blow job. But the prostate comment had Cam changing tactics. If anything should be tickling his mate's insides it should be his cock, not some lump of silicone. He reached down with his free hand, feeling across the curves of a plump rump, seeking for what shouldn't be there. *Found it.* And damn, Fergus's hole was snug around the plug. Cam felt the slick of lube around the hole and wanted to laugh. His mate had been sitting there all that time, painting his nails. *No wonder he started talking about sex.*

"Please." A thud sounded. Fergus was pounding the counter with his fists. "I need you. Gods, get inside me please."

Cam kept his mouth busy while his hands made quick work of his jeans, and the plug. Dropping the offending item on the floor, he shoved his jeans part way down his thighs, giving enough room for his cock and balls to be free. The single serve lube packet he always carried was slathered over his length in quick order and then with one final lick, he let Fergus's cock slip from his lips and straightened up.

"There's no going back from this," He warned as he lined his straining length up with Fergus's softened hole. Truth be told, he was just as eager as his mate.

"I know." Fergus was almost screaming. "Get on with it."

Oh fuck, heaven. Cam pushed forward. Fergus's body took him in and held him tight as though it'd been waiting for him. Perfect pressure. Just enough lube left so Cam could slide on home. Looking down, Cam took in Fergus's flushed face, the plaster of black curls on his forehead and the sweet torso also beaded in sweat. *Perfect mate.*

Their eyes locked, just for a moment, but it was enough for Cam to know his mate was as eager for their claim as he was. Gripping Fergus's outspread thighs, he started to move – long, sure strokes, his eyes never leaving Fergus's face. His mate was so open, so innocent. Cam's stony heart cracked open, his animal side already bristling with protective instincts evident in shifters everywhere from the beginning of time.

Cam knew, as his thrusts got harder, that he would work his ass off to make sure his sweet and precious mate was protected from the evil he'd witnessed for all their days. He would make his mate smile. He would keep his mate safe. He would... he would...

Fergus tilted his head, arching that slender neck that was screaming for Cam's marks. As much as Cam didn't want the moment to end, his balls were already tightening and the pit in his belly let him know he was so close. When his fangs dropped, Cam knew it was over and pushed by instincts not entirely his own, he bent over, shoving his dick as hard as he could into Fergus's pliant body.

One bite. Fergus's taste and emotions flowed through the blood that followed. Cam grunted against the skin, his spunk pulsing deep inside his mate, marking Fergus for all eternity. From the new smell filling the kitchen, overpowering the scent of food, he knew that Fergus had reached his climax too.

Carefully withdrawing his fangs, Cam tilted his neck just a tiny bit. He wasn't sure if a bull shifter would want to bite, but a brief sting on his neck gave him his answer. His whole body jolted, a second orgasm following before the first had even finished and as he closed his eyes, gently licking across the wound that would be scarred by morning, Cam could see his proud and stroppy animal, greeting the placid bull with a gentleness unheard of among the males of his kind.

It was done. Cam would never be alone again, and he vowed on his animal spirit that Fergus would never regret taking him as a mate. *Gods, I could stay here forever,* he thought, still lying prone over Fergus's heated body, the smell of their arousal still perfuming the air. But... *What the hell is that fucking noise?* Cam pushed himself up, his eyes seeking out the intruder.

"It's the oven timer," Fergus grinned, his face still flushed and his eyes gleaming. "I think the dinner's done."

As far as Cam was concerned, their dinner could burn to a crisp. He hadn't kissed his mate yet and that just wasn't right considering they were now bound together for life. Brushing back Fergus's errant curls, Cam leaned back down and cemented their mating with a passionate kiss.

Chapter Eleven

Phone calls in the middle of the night were never good news. No one ever rang and said "hey, you've just won twenty million dollars on the lottery," in the middle of the night. It was never positive, unless a family member was calling up to scream the good news about a baby's birth perhaps. But Cam wasn't close to anyone pregnant and the feeling of dread that hit his gut as he reached for the vibrating phone told him the call wasn't going to be a pleasant one.

A glance at the screen. Withheld. *It's not about the bar then*. Cam debated for all of two seconds before accepting the call. "What?"

"You know, friends are a weakness."

"Not if they're good ones," Cam said shortly. He should have known Austin wouldn't leave him alone without having the last word. "Your jackals didn't find anything on the bull. Your stooge was run out of town. What's next? A well-placed bomb to attract my attention?"

The huff over the phone was loud and angry. "Yes, well that's what comes of having imbeciles under you. Those jackals were meant to bring me the bull, not shove him out of a window. Noisy idiots can never do anything right. Let's get to the bottom line. What do you want?"

"I don't want anything from you." Cam looked over to see Fergus was watching him and managed a half smile. "I'm not even going to say I want you to leave me alone, because that in itself constitutes a deal and we both know how good you are at breaking them."

"It's one job. Purely personal."

"You've got a hundred men on your teams who can do just as good a job."

"Not in this instance, I don't." Austin hesitated and Cam wondered what he wasn't sharing. "There's a guy... he's gotten persistent and it's causing me no end of problems... I need him gone."

Cam stared at the phone in shock. "A mate?"

The silence went on for so long, Cam thought Austin had disconnected, but the time indicator was still showing the call was active. Finally, Austin said, "Do you know why you're my best killer? Because you don't have a heart. Because your type of shifter is gung-ho, go after anything and aren't afraid of any other living being. Heartless, fearless, with no respect for romantic ties. You wouldn't acknowledge your own mate if they came up and bit you and if they did do that, you'd still walk away."

Fergus slapped his hand over his mouth, his eyes gleaming

with mirth in the dull light. *You'd better not,* he mouthed, his lips still upturned.

"Thank you for your ringing endorsement of my skills," Cam said drily. "What you seem to forget is that not all people conform to their animal type." He had a lightbulb moment. "Is this guy wearing your bite?"

"That's not important." *Jackpot.* "I have other commitments, prospective family commitments that render this person a highly problematic nuisance."

Cam chuckled. "Okay. You say this man is wearing your bite mark, your permanent mating scar, and you want me to kill him. Is that right?"

"Yes," Austin huffed.

"He definitely has the mark? You haven't just given him a hickey?"

"He has my mating mark on his left shoulder."

Cam winked at Fergus who was following the conversation closely. "Sure thing. Send me the details. I'll do it for you, no charge."

Fergus's eyes widened so far, Cam thought they would fall out. He silently shook his head and lifted a finger, warning his mate to stay quiet.

"Good. Good. I knew I could rely on you." Then Austin must have finally clicked something was wrong. "Wait. Why are you being so accepting of this job, when you've never taken any other I've offered you?"

"I have my reasons." Cam chuckled. "Let's just say, I'll be getting more out of this job than you think."

"You said you'd do it for free."

"Uh-huh." Cam could see when Fergus finally twigged what was going on. "You won't have a problem with my checking to see the potentially dead man has that mating bite before I kill him, do you? Only, you know damn well, I won't kill an innocent."

"Why do you keep going on about the damn mark? I told you. We're mated. Double claimed if you must know. I couldn't help myself – damn mating pull – and then when I bit him, it turned out he bit me too. But he turned up at the wrong time, and the damn man was talking about moving in, and giving parties for... whatever. It's not your concern. I just want you to do the job."

"And you fully accept all consequences?"

"What consequences? Damn it. He'll be dead, I can have the offspring that my father's will insisted on. Do you know the fucking lawyers are holding out on paying me my inheritance because I haven't got any kids?"

Cam couldn't help it. His laughter bubbled out of his mouth, and he doubled over, trying to stop it. A roar of rage came from the phone and Cam slapped his chest a few times, to try and get his amusement under control. "Oh, my gods, so funny. Just too funny for words."

"How dare you laugh at my predicament." From the tone, Austin was seething. "It's no laughing matter. You know how the Fates are. I can't even get it up for a woman since I met the damn man, let alone service one, not with my mate still living."

"And you never will again." Cam shook his head. "It's fine. I'll kill him. Innocent or not, he'd be better off dead than mated to you. And besides, once he's dead, you will be too and that means you will finally leave me alone. Why? Because you will be dead, which is worth repeating. I don't even have to come near you for it to happen. You have a double claimed true mate bond. You'll die of natural causes within a week of burying him. It seriously couldn't happen to a nicer guy."

"Stop bullshitting me. You've developed a fucking conscience since you left the military and you're making up a whole stack of bullshit to try and get me to back off. There's no way the Fates would tie two shifters together for life just because of a few misplaced bites."

"If you believe that, then send me this man's details. But you might want to think about how you're feeling right now. You first got in touch with me about this, what, three days ago? Four? And I assume you haven't seen your mate in that time. In fact, knowing you, you shifted your fat ass the moment the claim was done and left him."

"So, what if I did. He was hardly suitable mate material for a man in my position."

"It didn't stop you claiming him though. You mentioned he's a shifter too?"

"Nothing of consequence. A cheeky little raccoon if you must know."

"Oh dear." Cam grinned at Fergus. "So, he's only a small guy, with a small animal spirit. I might not even have to kill him for you, not if you've left him to his own devices for the past four days." His chuckle was low and nasty. "It's time to start getting your affairs in order, Austin. You haven't got long left to live."

"Stop saying shit like that. If he dies I can..."

"He's going to die. I'd be surprised if he's still breathing, little guy like that must be made of strong stuff. But he will die, if you don't find him. Don't worry. Your thick-skinned rhino will let you know when that happens. Of course, by then, you'll barely be able to get out of bed for the grief. You'll be in so much pain you'll wish you would die. Hell, you might even put a bullet in your own head – make sure it's a big one."

"I don't feel any different." The words were laced with uncertainty.

"Are you sure about that? When two shifters claim each other their life threads are entwined for all eternity. That is why shifters are so protective of their mates. If your animal side doesn't go feral once the little guy is dead, in which case someone will have to put you down, your rhino will pine, he will die and when that happens, you will too. It doesn't matter that you're bigger and stronger than many. It'll just take you longer, but his death signs your death warrant. There's no cure. There's no way out. It's only a matter of time."

"You're wrong. You have to be wrong. He's only little... he, shit, he can't defend himself. He's a party planner." Austin was blustering now. "What if he... I can't... the Fates wouldn't..."

"Yes, they would. And if you don't believe me, just hop on the shifter council website and see the evidence for yourself. It's under the children's information about a mating. You signed your death certificate the moment you walked away from your future. Without him, you don't have one at all. At least you won't be pestering me with calls ever again. Have a nice death, asshole." Cam took great pleasure in ending the call.

Fergus was lying back, the sheets pushed down, his lovely body on full display, his full cock hard and leaking. "You're quite a nasty bastard when you want to be, aren't you?"

"Only to the people who piss me off." Tossing his phone on the bedside cabinet, Cam leaned into his mate's open arms and pressed his lips against Fergus's plush full ones. Being with Fergus was everything he could ever dream of. Cam gave a passing thought to Austin's mate. *I sure hope you've got a spine of steel little one, wherever you are. You're going to need it.*

Fergus pulled away from the kiss first. His skin was warm, the arms around Cam's neck solid and they felt so right. "You wouldn't have really killed Austin's mate, would you?"

Cam shook his head. "I would have gone to find him if I didn't think Austin's doing that right this minute. I'd try to help him, but the only time I've ever known a shifter to survive the death of a true mate is if the surviving partner has young children. Legend has it, the Fates entwine the fated mates' life threads so that they can reincarnate together into another life after death."

"I feel sorry for Austin's mate," Fergus said quietly. "From what you've told me, Austin has no heart, and yet he tried to claim you didn't either."

"Austin had better find his and fast," Cam said. He hesitated a moment, he found it difficult to share secrets, even with his mate. "Shifters know not to cross me. I can be lethal when I'm angry, and I won't apologize for that. But I've never killed anyone who didn't deserve it, even if I'd been ordered to. The only reason I asked Austin for his mate's details was so I could find him quicker."

"How can you tell? If a person's innocent or not?" At least Fergus wasn't running screaming from the bed.

"A shifter knows, hon." Cam gently stroked down Fergus's fine face. "One of the first lessons I learned after I shifted for the first time, was to trust my animal spirit. He is a stroppy bastard; I'd be the first to admit it. But there's a line no shifter should ever cross, and killing innocents is mine."

Fergus's eyes searched his and Cam let him. His animal had nothing to fear from the gentle bull, and he didn't feel challenged by him either. "Would you... would you still want me as your mate if I wasn't as innocent as you think I am?" he asked softly.

There goes my spidey senses tingling again. Cam thought for a long moment before answering. "We all have stuff in our past we wished we'd never done. That's the nature of our beasts, it's the nature of life. But the moment I saw you, my animal told me you were as sweet and as innocent a man as I could ever hope to meet. And I just told you, I trust my animal, and... I trust you too."

"I will tell you," Fergus said, and Cam saw pure hope shining in his eyes. "Just, if it's all right, not yet. Not here, in our bed, on our claiming day. Please?"

The cynical part of Cam's nature wanted to demand the knowledge now – shake it out of his mate if necessary. Secrets had the potential to cause problems – problems, Cam couldn't protect his mate against if he didn't know their nature. But his animal side wasn't perturbed, and Cam meant what he said about trusting him. And besides, Fergus's skin was so warm against his, and the sweet scent of their arousal perfumed the air. "Tell me when you're ready," Cam said gruffly, leaning down for another kiss.

Chapter Twelve

Fergus let himself into the back of his bakery, hung the keys on the hook beside the door, and then slumped on the long counter that ran almost the full length of his kitchen area. It was three AM on Monday morning, the air was humid, and Fergus was exhausted. But the empty cabinets in his shop wouldn't fill themselves and the construction workers would be in at six thirty for his breakfast creations.

"I need a boost of fabulousness," he sighed, glad there was no one else around that early in the morning. Snagging his apron from its hook on the back of the door, he slipped it over his head, tying the ties firmly behind him. "Bread first. Buns. Cinnamon, I think. Time to work."

It wasn't easy. Cam proved to be an energetic lover with the stamina any bull would envy. Whether it was Austin's early morning call that set his mate on edge, Fergus wasn't sure, but the two men had barely left their bed the whole of Sunday. Fergus was only glad their last bout had been in the shower. He didn't want the sound of running water to wake his heavily snoring mate. But as Fergus mixed, and kneaded, pounded and shaped his loaves, buns and pastries, he couldn't get Cam out of his head, or more specifically, when to tell Cam his secrets.

Cam can be trusted. Fergus knew that soul deep but that didn't mean he wasn't still worried about how his mate would take his confession.

I should talk to my momma first. It's not only my secret to tell. Fergus even pulled out his phone to do exactly that, but as soon as the phone was in his hand, he knew he wouldn't be making the call. The only time his momma was free to talk was Saturday mornings. For twenty-five minutes. The length of time it took for the washing machine to finish it's cycle, the noise of the machine meaning she could slip away and wouldn't be overheard. To call at any other time could put his momma in grave danger.

The kitchen started to smell of the delicious creations Fergus was pulling out of the oven. Fergus was moving like an automaton, his years of training cell deep, allowing him to move around the kitchen, creating the goods that would stock his cabinets. Platter after platter, Fergus actually jumped when the shop bell rang. He was busy filling the cabinets in the shop.

"It's only me," Sarah said brightly as she pulled her key out of the front door, a hulking wolf standing behind her. "Is it okay if Pierce comes in, only I promised him you made the most amazing egg muffins for breakfast and we slept in and didn't have time for breakfast."

Fergus's smile was automatic. Young Sarah looked very fetching with her bright rosy cheeks and the hint of beard rash around her chin. "I heard you'd found your mate, sweet Sarah. I'm surprised to see you here at all, but come in, come in. You should know your mate is always welcome. But as you can see, I'm swamped and the bar wants a regular lunch order as well, so..."

"I'll make us breakfast then get started," Sarah said, surprising Fergus by coming over and hugging him tight. Even the wolf's growl didn't seem to upset her. "I'm so glad you weren't permanently hurt by flying out the window."

"I'm fine, sweetness, and it's all thanks to you." Fergus

patted her on the shoulder. "You did exactly the right thing and isn't it romantic? Running into the bar to speak to my mate, and your mate is right there."

"I know." Sarah squealed and while Fergus didn't mind the noise, Pierce winced. "My mom always told me wolves could be so bossy, but Pierce isn't like that at all."

Fergus chuckled while Pierce looked up at the ceiling, his cheeks going a dark red. "I'm sure your mate is a wonderful man who has been bowled over by your Sensationalism. Now, I need to cook. You need to eat." He glanced up at the clock above the door shocked to see it was after six. "We have construction workers due in twenty-three minutes, and if you don't want to miss out..."

"We'll hurry." Sarah dashed into the kitchen, presumably to get some plates.

Pierce lingered and Fergus tilted his head slightly, his smile still fixed. "Are you a local," he asked quietly, "or do I have to find a replacement for my Sensational Sarah?"

"I come from all over. I own a trucking company. I'm happy to stay with her," Pierce had a low voice with a rumble indicative of his kind. "It's just, you know, people talk at the bar and well, I'll just come out and ask. Is this town safe?"

"Very," Fergus said firmly. "Look, I haven't been here very long myself, and I haven't even been to my mate's bar yet, but for the most part the people who live here are hardworking and they care about their neighbors. Ra, the tiger is a decent mayor, and Rocky and Mal run the sheriff's office like a well-oiled machine."

"But you had intruders in your home; Sarah said so. Is she

safe working here?" Pierce pointed at the floor.

Leaning against the door frame between the kitchen and shop front, Fergus ran a hand through his hair. "I know I don't look like much, but if sweet Sarah was ever in any danger at all, I would shift and let my bulk smash this place to bits to keep her safe. What happened over the weekend was an anomaly, nothing to do with this place. The intruders were from out of town and a onetime thing."

Pierce had the grace to look shame faced. "My apologies. I wasn't doubting your abilities. This being mated is all new to me. I haven't got a clue what I'm going to do if I have to do a long-haul run. Sarah loves her job."

"And I love having her here, but if you need to be gone for more than an overnight, then take her too. Mopey wee rabbits, even cute ones, are not good for business." Fergus smiled to show he was teasing. He pushed himself off the door frame. "Seriously, though, just keep me updated. Sarah has been training her brother Tommy to work here, and if I have to employ more people to cover for her when she's with you, I'm sure Sarah has other relatives looking for part time work. If she doesn't, Mrs. Hooper will know someone."

"That's good of you, man. I truly appreciate it." Pierce did look relieved. He looked around, noticing the people already crowded by the front door. "I might as well help out while I'm here. Did you want me to take the till while Sarah's making breakfast for us? I got a crash course on Cam's one on Saturday."

"Go for it. All the buttons are marked," Fergus grinned. "But put a smile on. We serve sweetness, light, and fluffy rainbows in this store."

"Smile. Right." Pierce showed his teeth. He really was a good-looking man, for a wolf. Of course, Fergus's tastes ran to shaved bar owners. Sighing as he thought of his mate, Fergus went back to his ovens. He still had the bar lunch orders to finish. *Maybe I can deliver them myself this time,* and that thought did perk up his mood.

/~/~/~/~/

Cam was in a mood. He'd heard his mate get up and go to work before the sparrows were awake, but as he'd been hard on Fergus's body during the prior twenty-four hours, he didn't let on he was awake, and in fact snored steadily until he heard the front door close. But the bed felt big and decidedly lonely with no Fergus in it and Cam struggled to get back to sleep.

His overly active mind didn't help. Cam had a lot to think about. There was Fergus's admission he had secrets to share from Saturday night for a start. Fergus hadn't said anything further about it, even though Cam gave him ample opportunity to talk. The lack of sharing was understandable in a way – it wasn't as though the two men knew each other that well. But it still niggled at him like an aching tooth. None of his research had shown any red flags on his mate at all.

But there was a more immediate problem. The fact they were both business owners. Businesses, that were quite literally like night and day. There had been times when the bar was busy with a celebrating group when Cam was only getting home at three in the morning; the same time Fergus went to work. Most nights he was home by midnight, but Cam needed to sleep just like anyone else, so it wasn't as though he could keep Fergus company in the mornings. And the bar opened at eleven sharp seven days a week.

Selling their businesses for either of them wasn't an option, at least not yet. Fergus's business was only new and from all accounts he was very good at it. Cam couldn't take that away from him. He could sell the bar, or at least appoint a manager to take over the bulk of the day to day. But then Cam tried to imagine himself in an apron, putting pastries and breads in bags and winced just thinking about it. *It would drive me nuts in a week.* Merging the businesses wasn't feasible either. Fergus needed the maximum exposure his shop front offered him, and his business catered more to family members, whereas Cam's bar was strictly an adult establishment.

With no answers in sight, and precious little sleep, Cam snarled when he saw Dave Hooper and his friends clustered around the bar's front doors. "I would've thought mating would have put you in a better mood," Dave said cheekily as he sauntered in before Cam got the doors fully open.

"Fat lot of good my mating does me, when my mate's business is three blocks down on main street and I'm stuck here listening to you guys gossip." Cam finished latching the doors back and cast a glance down the road. A woman and two small kids were just coming out of Fergus's shop. She was clutching paper bags as if they were gold, the kids jumping up with grabby hands trying to get at them.

We'll work it out. We have to. Cam stomped into the bar. He could pour drinks in his sleep and it wasn't as though Dave and his cronies ever ordered anything different unless they'd come into some unexpected money. Cam had learned to call Mrs. Hooper if that ever happened.

Pierce's two friends from Saturday came in, looking for a drink and food. Letting them know the food was on its way, the two men were happy to take the bottled drinks they ordered, wandering over to the pool tables getting set up to play. The little pool shark Roger came in, but he took one look at the wolves by the pool tables and scurried out the door again. That was unusual enough to spark Cam's interest, but he figured Roger had probably conned the wrong wolves.

Rocky strolled in ten minutes later, wearing his full uniform, his thumbs tucked into his belt.

Cam watched as Rocky scanned the customers, nodding at Dave and his friends before sauntering over to the bar counter. "Rocky." Cam held up a bottle.

Looking around, including over his shoulder at the open door, Rocky leaned over the counter. "Is it here yet?" He whispered.

Cam didn't have a clue what the wolf was talking about, but he leaned over the opposite side of the counter. "Is what here? You're acting like you're doing a drug deal, badly I might add."

"The food." Rocky mouthed fiercely.

"Oh," Cam stood upright again, "If you mean the food from Fergus's bakery..."

"Shush. Shush," Rocky whispered urgently, his eyes darting towards the door. "Mal doesn't know I'm here."

It was rare to see one wolf without the other and that was enough to keep Cam intrigued. "Rocky," he said quietly, leaning so no one else could hear them. "You could walk up to the bakery yourself. It's just up by Mrs. Hooper's store. You must have seen it."

"I know where the store is," Rocky hissed. "I just can't be seen going in there. Apparently, Mal thinks I ate the whole box of the eclairs he bought for the guys at the office, and he said I was getting fat. Me. Fat. Can you believe it?"

Having witnessed Rocky's appetite on Saturday, Cam could definitely believe the eating side of things. "So how did you manage to sneak out?"

"I told Mal, seeing as he thought I was getting fat, I was going to walk patrols this morning. I've been walking around for the last hour waiting for you to open."

"You could have saved your feet. The food doesn't get here until…, oh, here it is now." Cam's heart sank when he saw Sarah trotting in, with Pierce her faithful shadow bogged down by bakery boxes.

"Sorry if we're a bit late," Sarah sang out with her usual good cheer, directing Pierce through to the kitchen area. "We'll put these on platters for you to sell as you need them. Poor Fergus wanted to come himself but he was just leaving when that Mrs. Laramie from the big house at the edge of town came in, spouting on about some huge customized cake she is demanding Fergus make for her daughter's wedding this Saturday. I hated seeing how his lovely smile wobbled."

Cam knew how Fergus felt. Every cell in his body was

demanding he go up to the bakery and kiss his mate until his smile returned. But that wasn't professional, and it definitely wouldn't help Fergus's reputation if he burst in and interrupted a custom client session.

"He's missing you." Sarah stood up on tiptoes so she could lean over the bar. "He's trying to hide it, but he's not feeling as fabulous as he usually is."

"I know the feeling, sweetie." Cam rubbed his chest. He hadn't realized how much he hoped Fergus would come until he didn't. "But your boss has got a new business, and I know it's really important to him for it to do well."

"He says he has to," Sarah said and then she looked over, seeing Rocky stuffing his face. "Mr. Rocky," she called out loudly, "I hope you're paying for all of those eclairs. There were eight of them on that platter when I left the bakery and there's none left now."

"Shush," Everyone in the bar all said in concert.

Rocky's face went bright red, his mouth still full of the last of the eclairs. Swallowing hard, he brushed off his mouth and the front of his shirt. "I was never here," he said haughtily, putting some money on the counter. "I was *never* here, and I'll arrest you all if anyone says otherwise."

Laughter followed the sheriff out of the bar, and after serving Dave and his friends, and selling some of the baked goods to Pierce's friends, Sarah and her shadow left, trotting back up to the bakery. Cam's heart went with them. *Tomorrow will be different because Darwin will be working,* he told himself, trying to give himself a pep talk. Because, honestly, just knowing it would be hours until he saw his Fergus again was enough to make him think of putting a for sale sign on the bar doors.

Chapter Thirteen

One week rolled into two, and while Cam and Fergus had fallen into a sort of routine, it wasn't enough, and the strain was starting to show on both of them. Fergus had tried staying up and keeping Cam company in the bar in the evenings, but when he fell asleep slumped over the bar counter for the second time, Cam sent him home.

The mornings were no better. Cam tried coming in around eight a couple of mornings, but Fergus was so busy they couldn't even share a kiss, so Cam agreed to Fergus's suggestion that he get more sleep. Of course, that meant he was ravishing Fergus's sleep-filled body when he finally got home at nights, which Fergus never complained about, but the rings under his eyes deepened.

The only awake time they got together was when Fergus closed the store midafternoon and headed down to the bar to spend a few hours before going home. But as he locked up his shop on the Thursday of the second week, he wasn't even sure he wanted to do that. He missed Cam with every inch of his tattered soul, but he was so tired. Finding his regular fabulousness took every ounce of energy he had.

But it was his only chance to see Cam awake and besides, Fergus went passed the bar, to get to his house. He tried, he really tried, but as he trudged down the slight hill to where the bar sat at the bottom of the main road, he could barely muster a smile for passer's by.

It didn't help, when Fergus went into the bar and saw the place was busy. Some kind of construction crew, he guessed as he recognized the clothing and some of the faces that waited for him to open in the morning. The new sheriff's office was being built after a bomb incident, and it seemed the mayor's office hadn't stinted on workers. His heart sunk as his chances of having a stolen minute with Cam disintegrated.

"Fergus, come and join us," one of his regular customers called out, waving his glass of beer and barely missing hitting the head of his one of his friends.

"Maybe later." Fergus smiled and waved, but he was scanning the bar area, looking for Cam. Nicky and Darwin were working the bar, but Fergus couldn't see Cam anywhere.

"He's in the office," Darwin said, pouring drinks and palming money as fast as it was coming. "A couple of official looking guys have been in there over an hour giving strict orders they were not to be disturbed. They don't live around here."

Fergus froze. *No one knows where I am and even if they did... I didn't do anything wrong.* But that didn't stop his heart from pounding double time, and he struggled to breathe normally. "I won't disturb him then," Fergus waved toward the door. "Tell him I came in, would you? I'll... er... I'll see him when he gets home." *If he even considers my place home. It's not as though we've had a chance to talk about anything.*

Without waiting for a reply, he strode out of the bar, and headed for home. He wasn't running, but he was definitely power walking. *It's coming. I know it's coming. I just don't have any idea what this will do to my fragile mating.* Fergus just wanted to cry with the unfairness of it all.

/~/~/~/~/

"It doesn't matter how many times you keep asking me the same damn questions, my answers aren't going to change." Cam was keeping his temper but barely. It was gone three. Fergus would have been in already; been told he was busy yet a-fucking-gain and had probably headed home. The anxiety in his stomach had nothing to do with missing lunch. Fergus was upset, and that was upsetting him.

"We've told you we have reason to believe Fergus Franklin Ferdinand is a person of interest in a number of matters." Cannel, one of the two council guards who'd interrupted Cam's lunch rush said. "As his mate, there must be more you're not telling us. You've been mated twelve thirteen days now, more than enough time to share histories."

"We're busy. I work this bar, he works in his bakery, and there's a whole lot of stuff you're not telling *me*. I don't understand how someone with a squeaky-clean history can be of interest to the council guard. Has he personally committed a crime, or been a party to one?"

Cannel and his off-sider Brown shared glances and then Cannel shook his head. "No, he's not responsible for any crimes or a party to one that we're aware of, which is why we haven't gone to him personally. The council doesn't deliberately ruin a person's reputation unless we have good reason to."

Cam snorted but kept his opinions to himself. He was well aware of how the council guards operated. "You didn't seem to have a problem with generating small town gossip about me."

The two men ignored his pointed comment. "You just implied you checked his history before you mated him. Why would you do that to a fated mate?" Brown asked.

"Call me paranoid. He was new in town and I've had enough problems with people trying to stab me in the back, well before he came along."

More exchanged glances. Brown leaned over, resting his elbows on his knees. If he was aiming for coming across as non-threatening and 'we're all friends here', he'd underestimated the power of Cam's bullshit meter. "Look, you've been with the guy now for over a week. Is there anything that strikes you as hinky about him? You can tell us. We keep confidences. Shit man, you were in the service, you know how these things work."

Cam rested his elbows on the desk, his fists evident between them. "I do know how things work. You've got nothing on Fergus, otherwise he'd be tucked up in a cell somewhere with no chance to call a lawyer. You came to me, claiming some sort of connection because I'd been in the military, hoping I'd spill secrets Fergus might have shared when we're in bed together. You're missing one big point. Fergus is exactly who he says he is.

"What I can tell you," Cam continued, "seeing as you're so damn nosy about him, is he makes the best eclairs in the country – you can ask Rocky the town sheriff about them. His honey muffins will give you a mouth orgasm. He has pet names for people like Sensational Sarah who considers him the best boss in the whole wide world. He has never said a cross word, claimed a hatred of anybody, or never failed to stop and give people the time of day since he arrived here."

The way Brown and Cannel leaned back in their chairs let Cam know they'd heard the same things. "If you're investigating his family, then investigate them. Fergus hasn't had anything to do with them since he was eighteen years old."

"So, he has talked about his family, then?" Cannel perked up about that.

Nothing except that one comment about his mother. "Nope. I checked his social media pages which you should have done. There are no photos of him with any family member after he turned eighteen, the legal age for a shifter to be considered an adult. He's gay. It happens. I'm sure you've come across hundreds of shifters who are kicked out from their group because of their sexual orientation."

"Look," Brown tried again. "We don't want Fergus. We're not out to cause any trouble for him. But there're things going on with his herd..."

"Fold," Cam snapped. "A Scottish Highland bull's herd is known as a fold."

Brown let out a long breath. "His fold then. They're on our radar, we're talking national security concerns, but no one from there will talk to us. From what we can work out, the only reason Fergus got away, or left, or whatever you want to call it, is because he's not a full shifter."

That was something Cam didn't know, and he had to wonder where the council got their information from. But he didn't let anything show on his face. "I've seen Fergus in his shifted form. He's a big bull."

"Some half-breeds can shift." Cannel stood up, and after a moment, Brown did too.

Cannel dropped a card on Cam's desk. "Talk to your mate. Encourage him to share more about his family and his life growing up in the *fold*, and when you learn something, get in touch."

Cam's expression was clearly saying "not on your fucking life." Brown tapped the desk. "National security, buddy. You've been on the front lines and have shown your loyalty to this country for decades. Don't let us down now. The fate of shifters everywhere could depend on it."

Yeah, yeah and yet you still aren't letting me know what Fergus's damn fold are apparently doing. Cam followed the men out of the office, through the busy bar and watched as they went around the building to where their vehicle was parked. Moments later a large black town car sped out, spraying up gravel as it headed out of town. *Fucking show offs.* The day Cam was impressed by lousy driving techniques was the day he booked himself into a home for shifters with Alzheimer's.

"Fergus was here," Darwin said, coming up beside him. "He looked like shit, and frankly boss, so do you.

"We've only had one full day together since we've mated, and that was just after Fergus broke his back after being pushed out of a second story window," Cam said, his jaw tight. "Now there's more shit and council guards sniffing around although they are quick to admit my mate has done nothing wrong."

"You need a break boss. You both do."

"Yeah, well, while I can get people to cover me at the bar, there is no one Fergus can get to cover his baking even a couple of days a week." Cam sighed heavily. He knew he needed to get to Fergus, but he was dreading the conversation he knew they had to have.

"What about Brutus?"

"Who?" Then Cam's brain came back online. "Brutus the bear shifter, living with you guys? I thought he was famous for his chicken wings."

"You've been listening to Rocky," Darwin scoffed. "I swear that wolf has all people categorized by his favorite food types. Brutus is a damn good cook; makes his own breads and sweet stuff too. Rocky's probably forgotten, because I swear his brain is always on his next meal, but before all the kids came along, Brutus used to have baked shit around all the time. It might not be as amazing as Fergus's but it would be damn close, and that young mate of yours needs a break, before he shatters."

Before our mating shatters, you mean. But Cam didn't voice his biggest fear, even though he considered Darwin a friend. "I'll talk to him. We'd best get back inside."

"*I'd* better get back inside, boss." Darwin pushed on Cam's back. "You need to get to Fergus. We'll lock up here; just go be with him. I have a strong feeling he needs you right now."

We need each other. Fuck. I hate putting more hours on Darwin. But Cam knew Darwin understood. The mouse shifter had resisted the need to be with his mate initially when he and Simon first claimed each other, because Darwin had this urge to prove he could be independent. But it wasn't long before he'd come to Cam asking for less hours, which Cam was happy to organize.

Another push from Darwin, which really didn't do anything at all given their differences in bulk, but Cam started down the street towards Fergus's house. *Our house, if I have anything to do about it.*

Cam knew Darwin had been right the moment he stepped into the kitchen. Fergus was sitting at the small table, his eyes rimmed with tears, a pile of tissues sitting at his side. His small smile was watery at best and Fergus's bottom lip held a hint of blood where he'd been bothering it with his teeth. But it was Fergus's words on seeing him that broke Cam's heart. "Do you hate me now?"

Moving faster than he thought possible, Cam had Fergus out of his chair and into his arms in the time it took to blink.

Cradling his weeping mate softly, he strode into the living room, settling himself on the couch, and Fergus on his lap. "There is nothing on this earth that could make me hate you," he growled. "Absolutely nothing."

Chapter Fourteen

Fergus imagined a lot of things when Cam came home, and yes, he'd guessed his mate would leave the bar as soon as he was free from the officials. Hatred. Anger. Disgust. A demand for explanations. But there was none of that. The only thing Fergus saw in Cam's gaze as he walked into the kitchen was relief and concern. A concern that was matched by his actions as Fergus was swept into his mate's arms.

Much later Fergus would blame his fresh bout of tears on being so very tired. He hadn't had more than three hours solid sleep since he'd met Cam and the stress of spending such long hours away from his new mate had taken a huge toll on his gentle bull who was still a herd animal at heart. Being in Cam's arms was a heavenly feeling, and Fergus longed for nothing more than to curl up and never face the world again. But he'd known, deep in his gut, as soon as Darwin told him about the "official" men visiting Cam that the time for sharing his deepest secrets was long past.

"I would have told you." Fergus sniffed and wiped at his eyes although he didn't look up. Just having the steady thump of Cam's heartbeat under his ear was comforting. "I promise I've never done anything criminal in my life. I can't help the circumstances around my birth. I didn't ask to be like this."

Cam's thick fingers, that had given his body so much pleasure even when he was too tired to think straight, were a soothing massaging presence in his hair. "Why don't you start at the beginning, and tell me what this horrible thing is, that had you thinking I'd leave you because of it," Cam prompted.

"I'm not a pure shifter." Fergus squeezed his eyes shut, wanting to block out the slightest trace of negativity. "I shouldn't even be in this town. No one would want me if they knew. I'm a fraud. All my friends will turn me out when they know. Deputy Joe or Sheriff Rocky will arrest me, or maybe both of them together. I'll be frog-marched out of town like a common criminal. Mayor Ra will post a huge notice up at the town hall telling people to shoot me on sight."

"Ra's mate Seth is a hybrid. He's half fae half rabbit."

Fergus stilled on Cam's chest, although he didn't look up. "Seth is mated to the mayor? Didn't the townspeople know about his half breed status before they voted for Ra?"

"Everyone knew and didn't care." Cam's chuckles shook Fergus's whole body. "Ra met

Seth when Seth was being hunted by his colony. Let's just say Ra's no slouch when it came to tracking his mate down, although Seth wouldn't let the tiger claim him before the whole sordid business came out in the town square. Alpha Simpson, the rabbit leader claimed Seth was unnatural because he's a half-breed lop-eared rabbit, told everyone he was adopted, which poor Seth didn't know at the time, and basically washed his hands of him."

"Oh no." Fergus's heart hurt thinking about a poor rabbit in that sort of position. Especially a lop-eared one that was so small and cute. "Did the townspeople run Seth out of town? How did Ra get him back?"

"The townspeople voted to banish Alpha Simpson out of town, especially after he and his son Gareth caught up with

Seth in the library one day and beat him badly. Gareth was only allowed to stay because Seth spoke up for him, and said his father was forcing him to do it. Besides which, Gareth turned out to be Barney's mate, from the library, and Barney offered to keep the young rabbit in check."

Fergus's head was swimming and he had to sit upright. Cam didn't look upset. In fact, he seemed perfectly happy considering the bombshell Fergus had dropped on him. "You're telling me, even though this Alpha Simpson person was a full rabbit and the leader of the rabbit colony in town, the townspeople voted to banish him and Seth was allowed to stay?"

"It's not what you are, it's what you do that matters in this town," Cam said calmly. "What Alpha Simpson did was wrong on so many levels it wasn't funny. Not only did he beat Seth and could have caused damage to his unborn cubs, but Simpson insisted the members of his colony only mate with other rabbits. He refused to accept same sex matings. He bribed the mayor and sheriff at the time, trying to get them on his side, but the townspeople prevailed and voted against him. That's the way it is in this town."

"So, everyone would have to vote on whether or not I'd be allowed to stay in town?" Fergus tried to work out what percentage of the townspeople he sold his baking to.

Cam's fingers framed his face. "Babe, I promise you, the townspeople only vote to banish people who do something wrong. It's part of our laws here. The whole town votes before someone is banished or punished for any wrong doing. Being a hybrid is just a fact of life. It's not a crime. You've got as much right to be here as anyone else who lives in Arrowtown."

"But I'm not a full shifter." Fergus couldn't believe it could be that easy. He'd carried his secret for years, made to feel ashamed about his heritage before he understood what the concept meant.

"You shifted the day I met you, into the most beautiful bull I've ever seen." Cam was so calm, so self-assured, but Fergus got a hint through their bond that he might have upset his mate slightly when Cam asked, "Why would you think you couldn't be accepted here? How could you think *I could hate you* for having a secret like that?"

"Years of social conditioning? I genuinely thought right up until two minutes ago, every shifter felt the same way my fold leader did." Fergus shrugged but Cam's facial expression didn't change. Wiggling a bit, to get more comfortable which wasn't easy with Cam's length distracting him by poking him in the leg, Fergus laid his head on his mate's shoulder, and took a deep breath.

"I guess it's time to tell you a story. Once upon a time, in a far-off land, a young heifer was enjoying her time at college. She knew there was a mate chosen for her, back at the fold, as was the tradition of her group, but no one knew about that at the college so she was free to have fun and enjoy life like any young shifter should."

"She sounds like a sensible young heifer." Cam's arms came around Fergus's waist and settled there.

"She tried to be; she really did. But this was the first time the young heifer had been away from the fold and her family. There were so many people around, human and paranormal alike. She joined groups, made friends, and over time she made a very special friend. She knew their relationship wouldn't be sanctioned by the fold leader, but she was young and in love for the first time..."

"These things happen," Cam said when Fergus trailed off, imagining his momma in love. "What happened to the loving couple?"

Fergus shook off his romantic musings. "The ending wasn't pretty," he said, his heart feeling like the lump in his throat. "The paranormal wooed her with promises of forever love and a bond. She was so excited, thinking she could leave her fold forever and share her life with someone who loved her as much as she loved him. One night, two others suddenly appeared in the room they were sharing, the sheets still damp from their love making. 'It's time to come home,' they apparently said, and the man just got up and got dressed. When the young heifer cried, asking about the promises he'd made, he laughed in her face. Said the babe in her belly would turn her into a fat cow he had no intention of staying with, let alone taking as a bond mate. He was still laughing at her when him and his friends just disappeared. She never saw him again."

Cam's head rested on the top of Fergus's skull. "I'm so sorry. Some people are just assholes. What happened to the young heifer? Did she go back to her fold?"

"She didn't have a choice. The college wouldn't allow her to stay when they found out she was expecting, and she had no money of her own. The leader was very angry, claimed no other fold youngster would ever go out into a corrupt world again. The mate that had been selected for her was forced to go through the bonding, but the young heifer became nothing more than an unpaid servant for the fold leader."

"And the baby from this union – what happened to them?"

Fergus took a couple of breaths to center himself. He'd spent a long time with his memories packed away and it hurt to bring them out again. "He was born into a world where the only safe place was his momma's arms, where the only words of love he heard were from his momma. He was shunned by the others and grew up never knowing why everyone around him was so mean to him when they weren't to others. It was only when he shifted for the first time, so proud of his lovely bull form that stood strong and proud among the others, that he realized the true depth of the fold's hatred for people of mixed heritage."

"Oh, hon. I'm so sorry." Cam's arms around him tightened.

"It wasn't so bad." Fergus took a shaky breath. "The leader was getting more and more demanding of the fold members, restricting when they could work, and what they could do with their money. His distrust of the world outside the fold got worse with every passing year. But momma was really good at squirreling away a dollar here and a dollar there. No one cared when I went out and got a job because I wasn't useful for fold security or anything like that. We scrimped and saved and dreamed of freedom under the big oak tree in the leader's back yard..." Fergus's eyes filled with tears.

"Shush, shush, hon. It's okay," Cam soothed. "What happened

to those dreams you shared with your momma?"

"Her bond mate smashed them." Fergus felt physically ill. All the feelings he'd felt at the time came back as though it'd happened yesterday. "On the morning of my eighteenth birthday me and momma were supposed to meet at the edge of the fold territory. It was only two miles walk to the nearest bus stop. I had a change of clothes for both of us, and the money we'd saved together. But when I got there, momma was already there, along with her bond mate, his two brothers and the fold leader. They were holding her so tight; they wouldn't even let me hug her."

"The leader wouldn't let her leave with you?"

"That's not what was said at the time." Silent tears rolled down Fergus's cheeks, soaking Cam's shirt. "The leader said he wasn't going to allow any member of his fold to be corrupted by the outside world. That shifters mated with shifters and because I was a hybrid and thereby cursed, I wasn't welcome in the fold. He said the moment I stepped outside of the fold territory I was permanently dead to them all and would be killed on sight if I came back."

"Your momma wouldn't have accepted that, surely. Why didn't she go with you?"

"She pushed me over the territory boundary," Fergus sobbed. "I thought she was coming with me. The leader pushed her towards me. I went to grab her, to help her cross the line, and she pushed me. I stumbled over the boundary and her mate and brothers pulled guns on me. That's when they dragged her away. She was screaming she loved me and to always remain fabulous. It took me five years of searching, to find a way to contact her again and when I did, it was only then I learned the leader had threatened to chase us both and kill us the moment we left the territory unless she stayed and tried to have more calves with her bond mate. I didn't realize she'd barely let him touch her the whole time I was growing up. Now, I have a half-brother and a half-sister I've never seen."

Fergus gave in to his grief then. The pain of being away from the only woman who'd loved him, the torture she'd endured just because she'd given her heart to someone who didn't cherish it, the life she'd led after he'd gone, all the pain she'd gone through for most of her life, all because of him.

Chapter Fifteen

Cam was a grumpy bastard by nature, and it wasn't often he got himself involved in the affairs of others. Sure, he'd been one of those who'd stood by Ra when Seth's integrity was questioned, and he was happy to hold the fundraiser necessary for Doc to get the precious ultrasound machine he needed, back when Simon was pregnant. He'd gone with the others as part of the rescue team when Simon had been kidnapped and been part of the rebuild and renovation when Deputy Joe's house had been wrecked by vandals.

He was happy enough to joke and listen to his customers at the bar, but he rarely offered a firm opinion on anything. For the most part, he felt people around him got caught up in stupid dramas that could be solved with one quick punch, or a drink – whichever was appropriate – and after the life he'd led, Cam couldn't be bothered to be much more than a spectator to other people's petty concerns.

But hearing Fergus's story, holding his kind, sobbing mate in his arms, brought out a need for vengeance Cam hadn't felt since he lost his friends on the mission from hell. His mind was already running over scenarios – how to get Fergus's momma back from the clutches of a cruel fold leader. The other offspring could be a problem, but it wasn't insolvable.

Cradling his mate, Cam rocked his body slightly, offering comfort as most would offer a child. There was nothing childlike about Fergus though, and Cam wondered if his incessant erection would ever go down. *Use your big brain, asshole. Think. Strategies. Who to call? We're going to have to steal her from the heart of a territory ruled by a paranoid man who's gotten steadily worse. Or...* Cam thought about Cannel and Brown. Maybe their visit was more fortuitous than he'd first thought.

While he'd been thinking, Fergus had been slowly pulling himself together. "I'm so sorry." Fergus sat up and Cam felt the sticky wetness of his shirt pressing against his chest. Even with a red nose and puffy eyes, Cam knew he'd never seen anyone more beautiful. "It just gets to me sometimes and I haven't heard from momma since that call I had from her on the day we met. She doesn't even know I'm mated yet."

"She usually calls on set days and times?"

"Saturday mornings, between eight and nine." Fergus swiped the tears off his face and sniffed. "She has to do the leader's washing then. She hid a prepay phone in the laundry and she can usually slip away somewhere private during the wash cycle. Twenty-five minutes. But she didn't call last week, and I don't know if she will this week either. Maybe someone found the phone, or maybe her duties have changed. She said that my Uncle Mervin had been ordered by the leader to quit his job as he was needed for territory security which makes it sound like things are getting worse. I'm terrified of what might happen to her if the phone is found."

Cam remembered something Sarah had said about Fergus working. "Is this why you always work so hard? Have you been putting money away because you've got a plan to help your momma?"

"Momma doesn't know I want her to leave. Well, she does, but she doesn't think it will be safe for either of us, so we agreed not to talk about it. But my momma is one of the reasons why I started the business in a shifter town." Fergus caught Cam's eyes. "It was my momma who taught me how to bake cakes and breads. She loved being in the kitchen. Being sent to the laundry was her punishment when I sent her money one time. She was desperate. The roof was leaking and that bond mate of hers is useless. But the leader found out, took the money and punished her for having contact with a dead person. I thought..."

"You thought...?"

"I thought if momma knew I had the bakery in a shifter town and it was doing well, I could convince her she'd be safe here. I bought the house, I work my ass off, putting aside every cent I can spare. But there's so many guards around the fold now and the leader controls everyone's every move. She never leaves the territory and I don't know how to get her out."

"How much do you know about the fold leader's activities?"

"Not much," Fergus sighed. "My momma tried to keep me out of his way when I was growing up and she doesn't say a lot about him on our phone calls because she knows it'll just upset me."

"But has he always been this controlling – like not allowing the members into town, or to talk to other people outside of the fold?"

"Always. Momma said it's gotten worse, or rather the things she tells me about the family indicates he's becoming a dictator. She said something once about him stockpiling weapons and food. He's restricted all members' access to their own bank accounts and has taken them over for himself. I thought when she told me that he was some sort of survivalist, preparing for the apocalypse."

Or preparing for war. Suddenly Brown's warnings about the safety of shifters everywhere didn't sound so farfetched. The paranormal world was no longer a secret. Humans and paranormals mixed in most places, although shifter towns were specifically designed as a place where shifters could enjoy their furry selves without fear of being hunted. But the peace between paranormals and humans was fragile and relied heavily on paranormals conforming to human law in human cities. If anything disturbed the balance... *the apocalypse is one way of putting it.*

"Babe, listen." Cam made sure he had Fergus's attention. "The men who came to see me today were shifter council guards..."

"Oh, my no. Did something happen to momma?"

"No, no, or at least, I don't know. They wanted to know what you'd told me about your fold, and in particular, your fold leader."

The furrow that suddenly developed between Fergus's eyes was cute. "Why didn't they come and talk to me? I would have answered anything I could. It's not like I owe him any loyalty."

"The reason they didn't come and talk to you is because you're a very sweet man. You've never done anything wrong in your life. They came to me, because..." Cam blew out softly. "They knew I was in the military; they knew I worked on special assignments. They hoped they could claim a connection with me because I used to follow orders and know how their investigations work."

"They'd better not have tried to boss you around, just because you're mated to me. No, not even for that. No one should tell you what to do."

Cam felt the warmth from Fergus's defense of him right through his body. "They didn't say or do anything I couldn't handle. They claimed they were protecting your reputation by not storming into your store."

"Like storming into your place of business is any better," Fergus said hotly. "But wait. How did they even know we were mated in the first place?"

"I recorded our mating with the council a week ago." Cam smiled. "I did tell you I did it."

"Last week, last week?" Fergus's quirked eyebrow was a cute look. "Was I elbows deep in dough at the time, or falling asleep on your counter?"

"You were half asleep on my counter, with a smudge of flour on your face." Cam ran his hands up the supple muscles of Fergus's back, staring into his mate's eyes. "I have missed you so much, missed connecting with you, talking to you, just spending time with you. I'm gutted the one time I have a reason to come home early is because of those damn council guards."

"At least you came. I wasn't sure you would, or if I should've stayed at the bar." Fergus's top teeth raked over his bottom lip. "Should I sell the bakery, or try and find someone else to run it? I mean, if momma isn't going to come here, no matter what I hope or do..." The bottom lip trembled. "Maybe it's time for me to give up my dream of working with my momma and concentrate on my mate."

"Oh, babe, no. No. No. No. No. No. We'll both get more staff for our businesses. Darwin told me just before I came home that one of his house mates Brutus might be keen on working in your bakery. Apparently, he's not as good as you, but close. And I can employ someone else as well. Darwin has limited shifts because of the twins, but Nicky is always keen on more work. He might even take over as manager. We will work this out."

Cam leaned his head closer, determined to make things right for his beloved mate. "Not only are we going to get more time together, but we'll get your momma out of that fold. I'll be with you. We'll talk to the council guards and if they're just full of shit, then I'll call other friends and we'll stage a fucking raid. I'll challenge the damn leader if I have to, but we are not going to give up on your momma. All right?"

"I just want her to be safe. If she was happy there..."

"You know she's not and if she's suddenly stopped calling you then the sooner someone gets their ass up there and finds out what the hell is going on, the better. What the fold leader did is wrong. He had no right to prevent your momma from leaving. Any shifter, in any form of group, has every legal right to leave if they want to. Humans know about us. There's no risk of exposing our secret to them anymore. The law is on your side, and if your momma wants to leave, then she can."

"But what if they come after us, both of us? Cam, I couldn't bear it if anything happened to you because of this."

Cam wanted to close his eyes, blinded by the devotion he saw in Fergus's. But he didn't. "Did I ever tell you how old I was?"

The shake of the head was minute. "I thought around forty or fifty years old, because you said you'd been in the military and you've been here at least ten years, but it's never polite to ask once a paranormal is an adult. We live so long as a rule, it's really not important."

"Darlin', I'm a hundred and thirty-five years old. I fought in both world wars. I've been a military man for the best part of eighty years, from as soon as I was old enough to sign up. There's not a branch of the military I haven't worked in and that's without including all the black ops and special forces assignments I've had over the years. I could have worked as a shifter council guard if I wanted to, even a paranormal guard, but I never wanted to.

When I walked away from the military, I wanted a home, and I found one here. Now, I've found my mate. If you think that a jumped up, paranoid bull shifter is going to take away the life I've spent over a century building, he can kiss my hairy ass."

Fergus was trying to suppress a chuckle; Cam could see it in his eyes. "You haven't got a hairy ass. It's baby-faced smooth and gorgeous."

"It might not be hairy in this form, but if anyone from your old fold comes around, they'll be seeing my hairy ass while I'm tearing out their throat. Babe, don't you understand? We have friends here. Can you imagine your old fold leader up against a tiger or a bear? Do you think Rocky and Mal are going to stand by and let someone hurt you, if it means you can't cook eclairs anymore? Deputy Joe is a

Texas longhorn – his mate, Doc is a damn Komodo dragon, for goodness sake. Liam and Lucien are gorgeous lions both mated to Phoenixes. We're a mixed bunch here, but we won't let someone hurt our own. And don't even get me started about the Hoopers. They'll stomp on anything in four legs if they cause trouble in this town."

"But why would they care about me?"

"Because you belong in this town, babe." Cam stroked back Fergus's errant hair. "This is our home, and in this town, we don't let anyone hurt those we care about."

Fergus's nod was brief, but Cam could sense through their bond the hope that flared in his mate. "We'll talk to the council guards, see if there is anything they can do. If not, we'll go for option B, but I promise babe, your momma will have choices before the week is out, and if she does decide to come here, she can take over some of the responsibility of the bakery and she can make her new home in my house, because I've gotten rather fond of yours."

"You want to move in with me?" Now, Fergus was openly smiling and that settled something deep in Cam's soul.

"Move in with you, love on you, and never let you go," he promised.

Fergus's smile widened and a slim hand traced circles around Cam's right nipple. Cam's butt muscles clenched as he felt the touch right down his body. "Let's swap the order a bit," Fergus suggested, leaning so his mouth was millimeters from Cam's chest. "Start with the loving first."

Chapter Sixteen

Thanks to his momma, Fergus had managed to maintain his bright and sunny persona for much of his life. He refused to give into anger urges, always conscious that his animal form was bigger than many. Every time he'd been knocked down in life, and that had been often since he'd been kicked out the fold, he'd reminded himself there was always someone around who was less fortunate, dusted himself off and plastered a smile on his face. He'd grown up, knowing absolute unconditional love, and while it gutted him to leave his momma, he'd always hoped one day they would be reunited.

Now, he had someone else who would love him too; who looked at him as though he'd hung the sun and the moon, and who'd vowed in his growly voice that he would never leave. And Fergus believed Cam; he believed that no matter what happened going forward, he would always have his mate by his side.

He felt like a wet dishrag, the crying, the outpouring of grief, exposing his vulnerabilities in a guttural way that made him feel ugly. But the desire in Cam's eyes was unmistakable and Fergus's body responded. Was he scared for his momma? Definitely. But Cam promised a plan and Fergus believed him about that too. Now he wanted that connection with his mate – a reaffirmation and a desire to be present.

Cam must have been feeling something similar, or maybe it was their bond. When Cam's hands slid down his back, Fergus sucked in his gut so those hands could move past his waistband reaching for his butt cheeks. Fergus moaned, his head tilted up, seeking

Cam's lips that were right there for him to taste. Letting Cam control their kiss, Fergus ran his hands over Cam's shirt, feeling the ridges of the muscles beneath. Reaching around, Fergus curled his fingers, scrunching up the bottom of Cam's shirt, searching for the hot skin underneath.

Time blurred, clothing was discarded, scattered over the floor. Fergus was naked, his body stretched over Cam's bulk, as his mate was stretched out on the couch, his nerves tingling at the slide of skin on skin. Kisses turned frantic, tongues and teeth clashing, dueling as each man sought to get closer to the other. Fergus could feel the slick on his stomach, both men's cocks primed and leaking. Running his hands up Cam's broad neck, his palms tickled by his mate's buzz cut, Fergus ground down with his hips searching for more friction, his legs restless. Cam's hands moved from his butt, kneading, clutching him, blunt fingers stroking deep inside Fergus's crease, teasing the sensitive nerves around his hole, but never penetrating. Even in the throes of passion, Cam would never hurt him.

They needed lube. As horny as he was, Fergus was determined his balls weren't offloading until his mate's cock was buried inside of him. Pulling off Cam's mouth, he pushed himself up, panting hard. "Lube?"

"Ugh," Cam groaned, his head falling back on the couch cushions. "My pants pocket." His chest was heaving, and Fergus was momentarily distracted by how Cam's flat penny sized nipples puckered up when he was aroused. "I thought you were finding lube," Cam grumbled when Fergus's hands moved to tweak the nubs pointing in his direction.

Flicking his hair back off his face, Fergus looked around his living room. "You must have thrown your pants somewhere." He couldn't see them. He smacked Cam's broad pecs. "Come on. I'll race you." Sliding down Cam's body, Fergus took the time to give one broad swipe of his tongue over their joined precome glistening on Cam's abs. *So tempting,* Fergus thought. On any other day with an 'a' in it, Fergus would be slurping on one of his favorite treats, but the lure of lube and a wide bed was calling him.

Pushing himself off Cam's body, Fergus sprinted through the house, his bare feet pounding on the stairs. He heard Cam grumble, the couch was soft and easy to get caught up in, and he was on the bed, spreading lube on his fingers and reaching behind himself before he heard his mate. Cam came pounding through the door, stopping abruptly, the heat in his eyes so hot, Fergus could feel it burning his skin.

"Please. Turn. I want to see." Cam's whole body trembled with tension, but he didn't move from his spot by the door.

Wriggling around so he was facing the headboard, Fergus stayed on his knees, but slid them wider apart, his face flushed at being so blatantly displayed. His cock and balls hung heavy between his legs, but he ignored them, reaching around his body, his fingers quickly finding his hole.

Pushing in with his middle finger, Fergus gritted his teeth. No matter how aroused he got, his mating was still new, and he'd rarely bottomed before meeting Cam. Breathing out, he waited until his body accepted the invasive finger and then pushed in a second. Cam was growling, coming closer and Fergus let out another long breath, pulled the two fingers out and pushed in with three. It wasn't easy, Fergus had a long lean torso, and he couldn't push in very far. He spread his fingers, squished inside of him, trying to loosen his inner muscles.

The mattress dipped behind him, strong hands running up the inside of Fergus's thighs. The lube tube, which Fergus was still clutching in his free hand, was plucked from his fingers and seconds later another, thicker finger pressed in alongside Fergus's own. A rumbling noise filled the air – more of a rough purr than a growl, but Fergus could feel Cam's possessive pride through their bond.

Pulling his fingers out of his hole, because Fergus's wrist was aching, he rubbed them on a towel, left on the bed from Cam's shower most likely. Resting his elbows on the covers, Fergus let his head and shoulders fall tilting his ass up. The purr/growl got louder.

"Just perfect." Large hands spanned Fergus's hips, holding him in place, not that Fergus was even thinking of moving. A low slap rang along Fergus's crack – Cam's cock. Closing his eyes, Fergus felt a drip right at the base of his tail bone. His whole body relaxed. Cam had him, he was safe, and his mate was so turned on, the air vibrated with it.

/~/~/~/~/

Cam didn't consider himself an ass man. He appreciated the swell of a body in a well-fitted pair of jeans as much as any gay man, front and back, but when he saw someone new his eyes went to the man's shoulders, their neck, and how clothing stretched across a man's chest. Fergus didn't have a big build, but his shoulder/waist ratio ticked all of Cam's boxes, and his slim neck, arched down and currently bare of curls, called to something primal in Cam's make up.

Leaning back on his knees, Cam groaned as his cock slid down Fergus's crack, the bulbous head leaving smears of precome and lube in its wake. Using his thumbs, he held Fergus's butt cheeks apart, letting his cock do the poking and prodding needed for it to find the right place. He pushed forward, just his hips for now, but the urge to fall over Fergus's prone body and rut like a dog was strong.

Slowly, slowly. Fergus is the bull, not me. But Cam could imagine the animal urges because he was feeling them. Any threat to his mating, no matter how small angered his animal half and brought out instincts Cam had never used. The pressure on his cock was immense, but both men had been generous with the lube. Keeping a steady thrust forward, Cam used his hold on Fergus's hips and the resistance against the top of his cock to judge just how far and fast he could go.

Bingo. His cock completely sheathed in Fergus's body; Cam looked down to where they were joined. The paler skin of the base of his shaft contrasted strongly against Fergus's red hole, stretched wide and tight around him. Cam could've come from the sexy sight alone.

Then Fergus moaned and Cam moved, because the one thing he would always be was receptive to his mate's needs.

A slide out just far enough for Cam's cock head to nudge Fergus's inner guardian muscles. Then back in, not as slow, because Cam wasn't a saint, but as he moved back and forth, he wondered how long he could go for. Just watching, seeing how easily Fergus's body accepted him; Cam was doing some butt clenching of his own.

Running his hands up Fergus's back and over his shoulders, Cam let his upper body fall, his hands landing on the mattress, his arms bracketing Fergus's head. His hips writhed, arching up and down, moving his cock, the actions causing a tingling sensation around the nerves of his own hole. It wasn't a rut – more like a sexy hip dance, working Cam's lower back.

"Beautiful. Beautiful. Beautiful." Cam was caught up in their rhythm, nothing pounding, more like two men dancing together. He kissed every part of Fergus's body his lips could reach – shoulders, collar bone, the tantalizing nape of his mate's neck. Curling one arm around Fergus's torso to hold their upper bodies together, Cam kept moving, sniffing through Fergus's hair, licking up the sweat from his temple and down his cheek.

"Could eat you all up," he mumbled, knowing their sexy time was almost over. Fergus was arching against him, mirroring every move, his head alternating between moving up against his, and dropping down again. Cam slid his hand, currently splayed across Fergus's stomach, down until he reached the base of his mate's cock. A gentle slide up the long thick shaft, and Fergus cried out, calling his name, his whole body trembling with the force of his release.

Cam needed the bite and he took it, his cock spurting in time with the blood that pulsed into his mouth. Just a swallow was all he needed – he wasn't a vampire, but he felt the threads of their bond thicken as his cock offloaded into his mate's body. *Mine,* he thought smugly, although he didn't say it out loud. After all, he wasn't a wolf either, but he definitely understood in that moment why wolves had an affinity with that word.

Chapter Seventeen

"They will have to come here," Fergus said firmly, turning off the mixer. "They can come around to the back door. Nobody need even know they are here, provided they keep quiet, but I've got a ton of orders to fill and there's no one else here to bake."

It was Friday, after what Fergus privately called his 'breakdown Thursday'. The renewed connection with his mate, a decent night's sleep, and Fergus was feeling more like his fabulous self again. Cam arranged for Nicky to open the bar, so he was perched on a stool at the end of the long baking counter. Ostensibly, he was supposed to be helping, but he seemed to spend his time between texting on his phone, and nicking pastries from the trays when he thought Fergus wasn't looking.

"They're not happy," Cam warned, looking up from his phone.

"They want to talk to me, not the other way around." Fergus flicked back his hair. "I'm all for saving momma, you know that, but the rest of the fold can take a long walk off a short pier. Sarah, Sarah darling, can you remember what color flowers Mrs. What's-her-face wanted on that wedding cake? I swear my brain is full of holes today."

"Lime green, burned orange, and bright pink." Sarah stuck her head around the door and shuddered. "Apparently, to match the bridesmaids' dresses."

"Delightful." Hurrying over to his large chillers, Fergus braced the door open with his shoulder, needing two hands to steady the cake. Five tiers high, instead of the standard three, it was heavy, but Fergus managed to get it out without letting the chiller door hit him on the butt as he moved.

"That looks and smells amazing." Cam's eyes gleamed, and Fergus quietly moved it further down the counter. He did not have time to make another cake just because his mate had a sweet tooth. "Why can't they just have it in white like it is?"

"Wedding cakes make a statement." Fergus grabbed the huge bowl from under his mixer, and deftly divided the icing into three smaller bowls. "Most people want flowers on their cakes – I love flowers. I just prefer it when they are in more realistic colors." Finding the necessary food colorings from the shelf behind him, Fergus doctored the three bowls until the icing resembled the three colors requested.

"Are you sure she wanted burned orange?" Fergus called

out again, grimacing at the bowl. "A nice yellow, or even a bright purple would look better."

"Burned orange." Sarah poked her nose back around the door. "Brutus the bear friend of Ra's is here. Shall I send him through?"

"Another one of your mysterious texts?" Fergus shot Cam a look that said they'd be talking later. "Sure, send him in. He might as well see what sort of a madhouse he's walking into."

Reaching below the counter, Fergus grabbed a piping bag and his tray of nozzles. Deftly spooning the lime green mixture into a bag, he affixed the nozzle and started piping. One after the other, a mix of leaves and flowers started appearing on the pristine white surface of the cake. Spreading them out, turning the cake board as he needed, Fergus was focused on his task. It wasn't until the green piping bag was empty, did he look up. Cam, Sarah and two strange men were looking at him.

"Something wrong?" Fergus looked at the cake. Every leaf was perfect.

"You have some serious skills," the largest stranger said. "I'd shake your hand, but yep, you're busy. I'm Brutus and can I just say 'wow'."

Fergus felt his cheeks heat up. "Thanks. I've had a lot of practice. You're the one looking for the job here, yes? How about you pull up a bowl and make one of your specialties for me while I finish this? All the ingredients you should need are in the pantry or the refrigerator. This shouldn't take too long."

"Now?" Brutus shrugged. "Sure. Have you got a spare apron?"

Fergus tilted his head towards the hooks on the back of the door. "Help yourself." He filled a second piping bag with the pink icing this time. "And you are?" He glanced up at the second man who was now standing with Cam.

"I'm Seth, Ra's mate." Seth's smile was wide and generous. He was seriously cute, even for a rabbit shifter. "My mom's watching out for the kids this morning, so I thought I'd share a ride with Brutus and meet you for myself. This place smells amazing."

"It's the baked goods. There's nothing nicer when it comes to smells, unless it's our mates of course." Fergus winked before he started piping the pink flowers, varying the sizes and placements so they complimented the green ones. He was vaguely aware of Brutus moving around his kitchen. The man was soft footed given his size, and Fergus appreciated the bear wasn't pestering him with inane questions but was looking for the things he needed for himself. That was a good sign.

Five minutes later, the pink flowers were done, and Fergus looked at the burned orange icing and wrinkled his nose. The cake looked beautiful with the pink and lime green. Fergus had never been a fan of orange, but the customer was always right, even when they weren't. He tilted his head, this way and that, studying where he could create the orange flowers, so they didn't detract from what he'd already done.

"You could do one big one, right here." Seth pointed to a large white space on the second to top tier. "And then maybe tiny little ones on the other tiers so the color scheme all ties in together."

"Do you bake too?" Fergus imagined what Seth's idea would look like, filled a third piping bag and started to create the flowers Seth suggested.

"I don't get a lot of kitchen time," Seth said with a laugh. "Between the kids and Ra's job, and besides Brutus is very territorial about his kitchen."

"It must be nice, having so many shifter types living in the same house." Fergus finished the big flower and was now adding tiny little ones around the base of the cake. Putting the piping bag down, he eyed it critically. "Can you pass me the little pearls in that jar above your head please?" He asked Cam who'd been watching him silently. Pearls in hand, he added one each to the tiny orange flowers, and a couple in the center of each pink one. "Done." He stepped back to eye his creation. The pearls were the perfect touch, helping the orange to blend with the rest of the cake.

"That takes real talent, that does," Brutus said. He was hovering by the oven, watching something inside. "Sorry, I don't know your ovens yet. You know how it is."

And Fergus did. Every oven, no matter what it said on the temperature dial heated differently. Brutus scored himself another tick in the pro column. "Do you want to give me a hand?" He asked Cam. "I'll display this out on the corner of the counter. The customer promised she would be in before we close and it could be good advertising, even with the unfortunate orange."

Hopping off his stool, Cam came over, but he didn't touch the cake board. Instead, Fergus found himself being turned, and pulled against a broad chest. Cam brushed a quick kiss on the end of his nose. "Did I have something sweet on there you wanted to eat?"

"You're the sweet thing I wanted to eat," Cam chuckled, his arms tightening around Fergus's waist. "I'm just not sure I've heard anyone call you fabulous today, not even yourself, and I didn't want you to forget just how fabulous you are."

"I've been busy." But Fergus blushed under the praise. "Hearing you say it means the world to me though, thank you. Now, can we...?" He pointed to the cake.

"Only because the council guards are coming in fifteen minutes," Cam said softly. "We're meeting them at my bar, no arguments please," he added when Fergus opened his mouth to do just that. "This place is rainbows and sunshine and it should stay that way."

"I can stay for a bit if you need anything done," Brutus offered, pulling out a tray of delicious smelling bear claws from the oven. He must have used the puff pastry Fergus kept stored in the refrigerator, because there was no way the bear could've made them in that short of time if the pastry was made from scratch. But they looked crispy, smelled wonderful and Fergus's mouth watered.

"And just a dusting of confectionary sugar." Brutus finished them off with a flourish. "They're done."

"They smell amazing," Fergus said honestly. "You're hired. Please bag four of them up for us to go. Cam and I have to go down to the bar, but I promise we'll sit down and have a chat about hours and pay and all that when I get back if that suits?"

"Awesome." Brutus beamed and Fergus could tell he was a handsome man under all his facial hair. "I really love your set up."

"I have a feeling I'm going to love your baking," Fergus said warmly. "Come on Cam, let's get this cake moved and then we can go and see about rescuing momma."

"Rescuing someone?" Seth piped up. "Do you need a hand, only there's Ra, Rocky, Simon..."

"If we need you, you'll be the first to know," Cam said quickly. "Come on, Mr. Fabulous, let's wow the citizens of Arrowtown with your lovely masterpiece."

"I'm still not keen on that orange," Fergus muttered as he bent to pick up his side of the cake board.

/~/~/~/~/

Letting his eyes adjust to the gloom, after walking in the bright sun outside, Cam scanned the bar, but didn't see anyone he didn't recognize. "I put them in your office," Nicky said, when Cam looked towards the bar. "They said it was private and you know what this lot are like." He gestured to the table where Dave and his friends were holding court, pretending their ears weren't tuned to Cam and Fergus's arrival.

Cam's nod was brief. Nicky knew him so well and had done the right thing. The last thing either he or Fergus needed was everyone getting their nose in their business. Keeping his hand splayed possessively over Fergus's lower back, he walked his mate through the bar, and down the corridor that separated the entertainment space from his office.

"You have nothing to fear," he whispered low enough so only Fergus could hear. "You're fabulous, amazing, and wonderful and nothing anyone says in my office will change that."

"You're pretty amazing too." Fergus inhaled sharply and then scrunched up his nose. "Wolves. Still, they have the best noses. Let's see if they'll help get momma back."

Pushing the door open, Cam's eyes narrowed as he saw Cannel had taken possession of his office chair. "Are you going to pay my taxes while you're sitting there, or just trying to take the upper hand in this conversation?"

"Brown farted," Cannel said easily, getting out of the chair. "I was taking refuge as far away from him as possible."

"You had the chili last night, too," Brown protested, but he made room for Cannel on the two-seater he was sprawled over. "This is our runaway, half-breed bull shifter, I assume?"

"This is Fergus, my fated mate, who's only agreed to talk to you, in the hopes of gaining his mother's freedom from his ex-home fold." Cam already didn't like the tone this conversation was taking. Closing the door, he ushered Fergus into the chair recently vacated by Cannel, choosing to stand beside him, rather than perch his butt on the desk.

"You haven't been very forthcoming with us. Why do you think the fold leader is a threat to shifter welfare?" Cam knew his blunt question wasn't something either guard had anticipated.

"You've learned something new?" Cannel recovered first. "Your mate has talked to you about the fold?"

"Cam's mate is sitting right here, and I have a tongue of my own. My mate asked you a question." Fergus leaned his elbows on the desk. "Why are you interested in where I came from?"

The glance Brown exchanged with Cannel was loaded. "We've had some reports," Brown said vaguely. "Rumors. Complaints. That sort of thing."

"That's not telling us anything." Cam glared. "Did you ever stop to think that the reason no one in the fold will talk to you, is because you have a lousy interview manner?"

"The purpose of this interview is for us to gain information about the fold from your mate," Cannel said sharply although he wouldn't meet Cam's eyes. "You don't need to know why."

"I do," Fergus said hotly. "I want to know, why after all these years, I'm suddenly a person of interest. My momma lives in that fold. I have two half-siblings I've never seen, living with her. If you want information out of me, then I demand you tell me why your investigating in the first place. Is my momma in danger? Has something happened?"

"Tell him," Cannel said to Cam and he had the audacity to roll his eyes. "Tell your mate that's not how an investigation works. You know how it is."

"I do know how it is," Cam said, incensed his mate wasn't being taken seriously. "I know how easy it is for innocent shifters to be caught in the crossfires of an investigation. I know how often innocent people are suddenly gone, disappeared without a trace, thanks to an investigation. I know where those bodies are, so either start talking, or get out."

Brown folded his arms across his chest. "We can simply arrest your mate, and he'll have to talk to us then."

"Make him disappear, you mean." Cam felt his claws emerge from the tip of his fingers. "You've got no right to do that. Fergus has never put a foot wrong in his life. If you take him, then you'll have to take me too, and the mayor of this town, and the sheriff and all the deputies as well. You'll have to take the old lady who runs the corner store, and Hazel from the diner. Then there's the snake-shifting lawyer, because you have to know he won't shut up if something happens to Fergus and nor will the doctor. The rabbits, the deer, the bears, the wolves and the lions – they will all fight for Fergus. Are you prepared to risk all that – the obliteration of this whole town, just to talk to Fergus?"

"Damn shifter towns," Brown snarled.

"Babe, it's okay," Fergus said softly.

Cam hadn't realized he was growling at the end of his little speech, which wasn't easy to do because his fangs had dropped. Fergus's hand on his arm helped, but not by much. If Cam had his way, the two council guards would be pushing up daisies somewhere by nightfall.

"Look," Cannel said quietly. He'd lost a lot of his flippant nature and Cam's animal side preened. "We just want information. Then we'll get out of your hair, and you'll never see us again."

"And what about my momma," Fergus said angrily. "Will I ever see her again once you've gotten your information? What are you going to do? Wipe out the entire fold when most of the people there have no choice but to do as they're told by their leader?"

"So, it is the leader behind this then?" Brown leaned forward eagerly. "He's behind the gun buys, the propaganda, and the enslaving of innocents?"

Fergus's gasp told Cam all he needed to know. His poor mate didn't know things had gotten that bad. And that meant they needed to act and act fast, because the one thing the council came down hard on was slavery. "Don't say anything," he said to Fergus. "These guys don't care about your momma. I'll call my friends. We'll organize the raid and get your momma out of there. If you want to talk to these two afterwards, it's up to you, but don't say anything now."

"I'll arrest you for impeding a council investigation," Brown stood, reaching behind him. Cam moved, but it seemed something in Fergus reacted faster. A huge plume of smoke came out of Fergus's mouth, followed by a rush of purple flames. Brown yelped, brushing at his clothes frantically while Cannel sat like a stone, his mouth open in disbelief.

"Precious, that's enough," Cam said quickly as the smell of singed cloth and skin hit the air. *Fuck, where did all this come from?* "We can't kill council guards."

"They're going to arrest you for protecting me." Fergus's voice was guttural, deep, as though coming from another dimension. "I won't allow it."

"Yep. I think they got that message. They're going to tell us all we want to know now, aren't you boys?" Cam stared the wolves down, daring them to object. "Sit, Brown. You're not hurt, well, nothing a shift won't heal. So start talking, and maybe, just maybe, we can pool our resources and get this issue with my mate's fold worked out *and* save Fergus's momma."

Chapter Eighteen

Fergus could murder a drink – make that two drinks. His throat felt scratchy and raw and he was frightened to open his mouth in case more flames appeared. He was still stunned by what had happened. One minute, he was sitting there fuming about the evasive council guards and then suddenly he was belching flames like it was an everyday occurrence.

He knew why he'd gotten so angry of course. The wolves threatened to take his mate, who was trying to protect him and help him save his momma. Even though his anger rose fast, Fergus was trying to suppress his irate animal side. The bull was too big to shift comfortably in the office and someone could've got seriously hurt.

But it was like as his bull spirit was being pushed back, some alien being unfurled in his belly – that was exactly how it felt. Like a being who'd lain dormant for years had suddenly woken up deep inside of him, filling his belly with heat, and his soul with a strong sense of right and wrong.

Arresting his mate was wrong, and the creature knew it. Fergus had felt his eyes shift, and they'd focused with intensity on Brown - the man reaching for his cuffs. Heat flooded his body. Fergus opened his mouth to take in more air and instead flames came pouring out. He had no way of stopping it, because he didn't know how he did it in the first place. But when Cam spoke, it was like the creature listened, and the flames died as quickly as they started.

Fergus risked a look up at his mate, wondering what Cam thought of his fiery burp. But if Cam was worried, he didn't show it. He was still glaring at Brown, making deals, insisting the men tell them what was going on with the fold. Fergus could feel the creature, it was still inside of him, lurking, watching, waiting, listening to what was being said. *I just hope no one asks me to talk. I don't dare open my mouth.*

"You have to understand," Brown said, glancing quickly at Fergus and then averting his eyes back to Cam. "This whole business with the fold is part of a much larger operation. We've been trying to crack down on a shifter slavery ring for the past two years. Little kids, aged between five and ten years old, being sold to extremely wealthy humans."

"That sucks but it happens," Cam said shortly. "The odd paranormal has been known to do the same thing to human children. One of my last assignments was taking out a vampire who'd run his operation for over ten years, selling children to feed coven members with a sick appetite. What makes this scum any different?"

"We raided one auction. It was the only lead we had at the time." Cannel looked down at his hands. "The kids were dressed nicely enough; they'd been kept fed and were clean, but it was as though there was no life left in their eyes."

"The council has counselors and therapists to help them get over the trauma. Being reunited with family would also help with their recovery." Cam's expression didn't change, and if it wasn't for the slight tightening of his hand on Fergus's shoulder, Fergus would imagine his mate unaffected.

"That's just it," Cannel looked up and even Fergus could see he was distressed. "There were no parents – all of the parents who'd reported their kids missing suffered an accidental death soon after the kids were stolen from them. It was as though someone was erasing the fact the kids even existed. And then there was something else..." He trailed off and Fergus wanted to stamp his foot in frustration. It was bad enough hearing about poor abused children sold into slavery, but the men still hadn't said anything about how this tied to the fold.

"All the kids we recovered had a computer chip in their brain," Brown said. "At first, we thought it was a tracking device, in case any of the children ran away from the people who'd bought them. But it was worse, much worse. The chips affected a part of the brain that rendered them completely docile, making it impossible for any of them to fight back against the people who bought them."

Fergus felt Cam's slight body tremor run through the hand resting on him. "Barbaric, I agree," Cam said curtly." But it's not like the military hasn't used experimental processes in the past to control people."

"This control was a long-term plan," Cannel said. "Our scientists got onto it, the moment we realized what was going on – removing the chips and studying them. From what they can tell us, the chips are controlled remotely, and they all had a switch. One minute, the child is docile, following orders as they've been programmed to do. The next, they become killing machines. They take out the person they've been ordered to kill, and the moment the job is done, a huge electrical surge is sent through the chip, killing the shifter youngsters instantly."

Fergus closed his eyes as the creature in his belly rumbled angrily. It was comforting that the being wanted to protect children, but Fergus didn't want to draw any attention to himself. Not when he wasn't sure how much control he actually had over his body.

From Cam's tone, it was clear he wasn't feeling any better. "How many of these children are there out there, in the community, ready to go off? And what the hell does any of this shit storm have to do with my mate's fold?"

"We don't know how many," Brown said. "When the auction was raided, we got some details, but they were sketchy. All we knew for certain was that the children were only sold to humans with a lot of money, who held important positions..."

"And whose death would create a public outcry among humans against shifters once details of how the person died was made public. I get that, I do," Cam said angrily. "But how did Fergus's fold get implicated in all of this? You're talking about a scheme that could have been in the making for a decade or more. People don't just wake up one day and decide to ruin the peace between the paranormal and human worlds in a master plan that could take years to come to fruition. You said yourself the kids you found at the auction were very young – they were years away from their first shift. They wouldn't be a danger to a full-grown human at that age. Hell, it could be humans behind all this, seeking to have paranormals contained in camps or something like what was suggested fifty years ago when we first came out."

"It's definitely a shifter operation," Cannel glanced at Fergus. "Three of the five guards we captured were Scottish Highland bull shifters, identified as coming from your mate's fold. They died, in custody, before they were interviewed. The burner phones we recovered all only had one number on them – belonging to the leader of the fold."

Fergus frowned. He wasn't overly surprised at his leader's involvement. Cannel and Brown wouldn't have been so persistent about talking to him otherwise. What he didn't understand was if the council had all this evidence, why hadn't something been done about it. "Why haven't you picked him up then?" He asked, relieved when nothing flammable came out of his mouth. "The leader, I mean. You have the evidence. It all points to him, or someone within the fold. Why have you been working on this for two years, and not done anything about it?"

"The place has become a stronghold," Brown said. "Barely anyone in or out. We've got no way of knowing what weaponry he has, or how many people are in there."

"The few times we have managed to capture someone, who's left the compound, they've ended up dead and not by our hands. Our scientists found remains of the same computer chip found in the children, in every one of them," Cannel added. "Do you see now Fergus, why anything you can tell us is so important? If every person in that compound has been fitted with a chip, then with one push of the button, they could all be dead, and we'd be no closer to finding out how many children are already living with their new human owners. We don't know if that's the case, of course, but we can't take the risk."

"They didn't chip me." Fergus ran his fingers through his hair, testing every bump on his skull. "They didn't chip me because the leader thought I was useless, because I'm a hybrid and he didn't want my genetics in the fold."

"You're the only person who's successfully left the fold and lived to tell about it." Brown looked down at his singed clothing. "Of course, I'd have preferred the other half of your genetics didn't come from a dragon, but there you are. That probably saved your life."

"A dragon?" *That's what's woken up inside of me?* "But, when my momma told me about my biological father, I thought from the way she described the men disappearing out of the room, my father was fae or a djinn."

"Neither the fae or djinn are capable of breathing fire, but many dragons have magic which is how the men might have appeared and disappeared the way they did," Cam said quietly. "Fergus, hon, I know this is super confusing and we've got a lot to talk about. But if we've got any chance of saving your momma, you need to tell these two everything you can remember from your life in the fold."

Fergus thought longingly about his bakery, and then about his warm comfortable bed. He'd rather be in either of those places than talking to the council guards, especially if Cam was with him, but it wasn't like he had much of a choice. Children's lives depended on it. His momma's life might depend on it. Just the thought of her having a computer chip in her head made Fergus feel sick. "Are you recording this or writing it down? This could take a while."

/~/~/~/~/

Cam hated how useless he felt, running around, getting his mate drinks, ordering lunch from the diner when it was clear Fergus was doing his best to tell everything he knew, but not able to do much else. Every word from Fergus's mouth angered him. How his fabulous mate was ignored, belittled, abused even, purely because he wasn't a pure bull shifter.

But there wasn't anything he could do about that either and it didn't help, that Cam had a sinking feeling that saving Fergus's momma, who'd clearly done the best she could for her loving son, wasn't going to be a slam dunk. If she had been chipped, as the council guards feared, then pulling her out of the compound before the leader was dead, could be a death sentence for her.

Hours passed. Sarah and Brutus called into the bar, Sarah with the bakery takings and to tell Cam the lady adored the wedding cake, and Brutus to let Fergus know he'd prepared the dough for the morning bread order. Darwin took over from Nicky at the bar, and Cam got five minutes to talk to Nicky about managing the place. He was keen and they agreed to talk more when Cam had more time. In the meantime, Nicky would be opening the bar in the morning and that was as far as Cam could think for now.

And still Fergus talked; everything he could think of, from the number of houses in the compound, to the fact that his Uncle Mervin had been told to quit his job and work as security for the fold. Everything Cam heard indicated the leader was far more than a paranoid nut case. He was a despot, a dictator with a long-term plan, and it would seem he had at least fifty people under his care, many of them children.

The curtains had been drawn and the lights turned on by the time Fergus finished. "I don't know any more. I'm sorry. But it's been years..."

"You did good, babe," Cam said quickly, daring Cannel or Brown to say any differently. "I'll see these two out, and then we'll head home, yeah? Have a nice hot bath and curl up with a movie. Gentlemen." He tilted his head towards the door and both men got the hint and stood up.

Cam waited until the pleasantries were over and he had Cannel and Brown in the hallway before he said anything. "Is it enough?" he growled. "Can you get Fergus's momma out safely and any other innocents in the fold?"

Both wolves looked uneasy. "We can't focus on your mate's

momma, you know that. We have to get to the leader, and anyone else in the inner circle who might be involved. This is going to take a full-scale raid, and while Fergus's intel is a huge help, we can't guarantee the safety of anyone once we breach that compound."

"Then take me with you," Cam growled. "You focus on what you need to do, and I'll find Fergus's momma and get her out. If Fergus's siblings are with her, I'll grab them too. I've got the training, you know I have, so don't use that as an excuse to say no."

"Cam..."

"No excuses." Cam pointed back at his office door. "That man has given his all in there today. He's tired, worried sick about his momma, and he just learned he can breathe fire. If that's not overwhelming, I'm not sure what is. He'll want to go with you. I'm not going to let him and I don't want to even think about what that's going to do to our new mating, but you will take me with you... or... do you need me to call one of my connections and force the issue, because I will."

Brown shook his head as Cannel scribbled on a piece of paper, ripping it off the pad and slamming it on Cam's chest. "Oh three hundred tomorrow. Be there or miss out. Once we enter that compound, I don't know you and I don't want to know you. You do what you have to do and get you and the lady out. Understood?"

"Understood." Cam showed his teeth. "Just like old times. Now piss off. I've got a rescue to plan."

Chapter Nineteen

Fergus knew something was going on with his mate, but he couldn't put his finger on what it was. When they got home, Cam was sweet, thoughtful, cuddling him close and somehow understanding Fergus was all talked out. They shared a bath, just as Cam had promised, the aromatic bath oils his mate used, combined with the events of the day, made him sleepy. Fergus didn't see the end of the movie Cam put on, and he only vaguely remembered his mate picking him up and putting him to bed.

Through it all, Fergus had a sense of uneasiness and it had nothing to do with the dragon he now knew was inside of him. It was like a nagging flicker in the back of his brain. Cam was plotting something, but Fergus couldn't get a handle on what it was, and he was too shattered to ask. But those feelings came flooding back when he woke suddenly from a deep sleep to find the space in the bed was empty beside him.

Animal senses, dragon and bull, let him know Cam wasn't in the house. Picking up his phone from the side of the bed, Fergus saw it was just after two thirty – in the morning – far too early or late, depending on how you looked at it, to be up and about.

Don't get upset about this, he warned himself as his heart started to beat faster and his old insecurities crept into his brain. *Cam is a shifter and a claimed one at that. He also has far too much honor to run out on you in the middle of the night. There must be a good reason. Think. Look for a note.*

Getting up, Fergus checked the bed, even lifting the pillows to make sure he hadn't knocked a piece of paper under there while he was still asleep. *Nothing. Okay. Hit the bathroom, then check the kitchen.* Cam knew Fergus always made a coffee before he headed to work, and as Fergus was due to be up for work within the next hour, Cam would know he couldn't just sneak out without his absence being noted. *Especially at this time of night.*

The expected note was propped up on the coffee pot which had already been filled, ready for him.

To my beloved Fabulous Fergus,

You're going to be pissed at me. I know that. But I also know those damn council guards don't give a shit about your momma – and that you do. I got them to agree to let me go on the raid of the compound – my only mission is to save your momma and I'm going to bring her back with me.

Shit hon. Writing this is so hard. It was never my intention to keep anything from you, but the thought of you facing your fold leader was more than my animal half could stomach. I'd rather have you yell at me, than have to hold you and watch you while you suffer, crying over your momma's needless death – and we both know that's a possibility.

I've done this before, countless times. Trust in me, please.

Love Cam.

"Oh, Cam, you damn fool. When on earth were you going to start trusting me?" Leaning on the counter, Fergus bowed his head.

/~/~/~/~/

Gods, these guys are noisy fuckers. Cam scowled as yet another guard brushed past him, intent on scaling walls.

There was no finesse involved in a council raid – it went exactly as the name implied. Battering rams on the compound gates, flood lights going up everywhere, while other guards scaled the walls, guns strapped to their backs like *Rambo* rejects. It was stupid, designed to create panic and Cam knew from experience that in that panic, the bad guys nearly always got away.

This time the fold leader wasn't his concern. Cam double checked his phone, memorizing the photo he'd lifted from Fergus's social media. The picture was old, but shifters barely aged after the age of twenty-five. The woman in the photo looked so much like Fergus it was uncanny – her hair slightly longer, and just without the facial hair Fergus rocked so well.

Think. If I was a paranoid fold leader and I had someone living like a slave, where would I keep them?... The basement. The choice was obvious as far as Cam was concerned. Sure, the woman was supposedly bond mated, but that was a forced pairing, so it was unlikely there was any love lost between the pair. It also bugged Cam that she hadn't called Fergus like she usually did, *which means perhaps getting caught with the phone and being punished for it.*

The panic Cam predicted had already started; women screaming, men bellowing, gunfire masking the sound of children crying. Cam was up and over the wall before anyone had noticed him, his spot chosen specifically because it was the closest to the leader's house. He debated shifting, but that would make it impossible for him to talk to Fergus's momma when he found her. Besides, if she was behind locked doors, he needed opposable thumbs. Moving quickly and silently, he headed straight for the basement window, which was exactly where Fergus had said it would be. The shadows and the confusion provided excellent cover.

The bars covering the window were a new edition. But a quick glance showed they'd been shoddily installed. Reaching into one of his many pockets, Cam pulled out a multi-head screwdriver, and got to work. He only needed two of the bars off – the rest could stay. He would have gotten them off faster, but he had to keep checking his surroundings. So many people were still in panic mode, running around with no fixed destination in mind – *Just another example of a council fuck up.*

The last screw was out, and Cam was just lifting the bar off the frame, when the wailing started, first one woman and then another and another. *Oh, mother of gods, please tell me that bastard hasn't activated any chips.* Cam's need to get into the basement intensified. Using his boot, he smashed the glass, kicking out the shards so he wouldn't get cut. He didn't even look into the darkened room; he just dived through the window, expertly rolling on the solid concrete floor in a way that had him back on his feet quickly.

Come on lady, please be here, please be here. If she wasn't, then Cam was going to have to make his way clear over to the other side of the compound, and that wasn't going to be easy with so many people around. Looking around in the gloom, all Cam could see was boxes stacked at least six high. Gun cases. Cam curled his top lip. The leader wasn't only paranoid, he was planning for fucking Armageddon.

Moving silently relying on his animal's keen eyesight, Cam sniffed hard. The smell of gunpowder and oil made it hard to pick out any other scents. Keeping his back to one wall, Cam moved down the rows of gun cases; there had to be over a hundred of them packed in rows. He was nearing the end, and hoping to find a door, when he heard a whimper. At the same time the sickly stench of blood hit his nose.

Oh, no, no, no, no, no. Cam scanned the aisles between the boxes. There, in the far corner was a heap of what looked like clothing, but as he got closer, he could make out the slender form of a person. A person who was bleeding heavily.

"Hello." Cam kept his voice low. Even though he was sure

any security would be too busy dealing with the chaos outside, it was always ingrained in him to be careful. "Are you all right? Do you need assistance?"

"Who... who are you?" The mound of clothing stirred, and a face appeared. Cam held back his gasp with difficulty. The face was so like that of his mate, it was uncanny – the same eyes, nose and the shape of her mouth. But whereas when Cam left Fergus's, his mate's face was beautifully relaxed and smooth, his mother's was covered in bruises, angry cuts carved in both of her cheeks.

Cam forced his facial features not to change. "Ma'am, you don't know me, but I'm your son Fergus's mate. There's currently a council raid going on upstairs, but that's got nothing to do with me. My only task is to get you out of here and back to Fergus."

"My Fabulous Fergus has a mate? That makes me your momma too." Momma tried to smile even as her eyes filled with tears. "You make sure you look after him, please, and tell him..."

"You can tell him yourself," Cam said brusquely as he bent to pick her up. But momma pushed him away.

"I can't go with you." Pushing aside the clothing covering her body, momma waved to indicate her legs. "I'll never walk again. He made sure of that."

Cam's gut clenched, and he took a few moments to breathe through his mouth. He'd seen some sick things in his life, but the sight of momma's mangled legs and feet ranked as some of the worst. The wounds were dirty, some healing, others looking as though they'd only been recently inflicted. But the broken bones and mangled skin meant momma was probably right.

His lips tightened. "I'll just have to carry you then."

"No." Momma leaned back. "I can't let Fergus..."

"Fergus is exactly the reason I'm not leaving you here to die," Cam said fiercely. Every instinct was telling him he was running out of time. "He's not going to care if you can walk or not. He loves you. He misses you and he's going to be damned pissed at me that I left him in bed and snuck out, just to save you. So, you need to be in my arms when I see him again. It's the only thing guaranteed to save me from his anger and disappointment and I'd rather piss you off than him."

Momma chuckled; the sound cut off as she grabbed her ribs. "The Fates chose well for my darling son." She lifted her arms. "Do what you have to, and don't worry about hurting me. I can keep quiet. I'm not going to let you and Fergus argue just because of me."

"Yeah, well he's just inherited fire breathing abilities," Cam said, hoping to divert momma from her pain. "I don't know who was more shocked, me or him." Wrapping the coat around momma's legs, he swung her into his arms as carefully as possible, before making his way back along the wall.

"Fire breathing." Momma's head flopped on Cam's shoulder. "I always knew his dragon side wouldn't come out unless he found his fated mate. That's why I never told him."

"You can tell him all about it when you're well." Cam had reached the basement window. Looking out, it was as if Armageddon had already hit the compound. Dead bodies laid strewn around, some in guard uniforms, while others were shifted bulls. What was more disturbing was the bodies of women and children lying dead without a mark on them. "The chips," he said urgently. "Are you fitted with one of those chips?"

"You know about them?" Momma shook her head. "No, he didn't bother chipping me. He'd already run Fergus off, and then he took the two other children I was forced to have. I don't know what happened to them, and I can't even feel sorry they're gone right now. According to he who shall not be named, I'm just broken and at the moment, that's exactly how I feel."

"Then we'll just have to get you fixed again. Hold on, this is going to be tricky." Climbing out of a window, was a lot more difficult than jumping in one, especially with the added weight in his arms. But Cam had spent decades training for just this type of moment, and he wasn't about to fail now. Free from the building, he eyed the height of the fence. It would be a lot easier going through the front gate, and with that in mind, he sprinted over to the fence, and started to follow it around to the front of the compound. The less time he had to worry about people surrounding him the better.

There were at least a dozen guards milling around the compound gate, and Cam hesitated. They would know his face, but Cannel and Brown hadn't said anything about him rescuing someone out of the compound. The last thing momma needed was to be taken away, interrogated, and god knows what else the damn investigating team would want to do with her.

Later, he would blame the stench of blood still coming off momma, and his intense focus on the guards at the gate for what happened next. "You'll do perfectly." A snarling voice sounded in his ear as the unmistakable shape of a gun barrel pressed against Cam's temple. "You're going to shut your mouth and start moving. Thanks to you and the mess in your arms, they're going to let me walk right out of the front gates."

"Oh, my gods." Momma's fingers clutched Cam's shirt tight and her head pressed closer to his neck. "Don't hurt this man. Please don't hurt him. He's got nothing to do with any of this."

"You always were too soft, Marybelle." Cam caught the edge of a sneer in his peripheral vision. "Walk." The gun pressed hard enough to leave an indent. Cam took one step, then another. He knew the moment they'd all been seen, when a shout went up and the sound of a dozen rifles cocking were pointed in his direction.

Scanning the faces, Cam looked for anyone among the guards who had an ounce of experience. The problem with shifter faces was they all retained a twenties appearance. So, the faces weren't a clue, but body language was. Cam discounted twitches, slouches, anyone who looked the slightest bit worried. Cannel appeared from the front of the house, but Cam discounted him immediately. He just needed one guard.

There, in the back, Cam saw a face he recognized, and held the man's eyes. He saw the flicker of recognition, a quick glance around, and then the man nodded, so slight it was easy to miss. Cam took another step.

"You won't get away Albert," Cannel called out. "The moment you stop hiding behind the innocents, you're dead."

"I'll sue you all for incompetence," the voice behind Cam was harsh and arrogant. "Council guards killing women and children. Planning a night raid in a family compound. My whole fold dead and for nothing. You've got nothing on me."

"It was you who killed the women and children. We've got the chips," Cannel yelled. "And the control app." He held up a tablet. "We've got the kids we saved from the auction last September, and the dead guards that came from your fold. I'll bet my life your finger print is the only one that opens this tablet and that makes this whole thing an open and shut case. You're not worth the cost of a trial."

"Then I've got nothing to lose," Albert cackled. "I'll take you all with me."

The moment the gun muzzle moved from Cam's temple he yelled, "E*t ad sinistram*." Holding momma tight against his chest, he dropped and rolled to the left. He saw Albert jerk as the guard who Cam recognized shot him right between the eyes, and the hail of bullets that followed left Albert's body riddled with holes.

"It's going to be all right," he whispered to momma who was shaking in his arms. "We're going to go home, and Fergus is going to cry, and laugh and ply us both with honey muffins until we're so stuffed we can't move."

"You won't be moving anywhere." Cam looked up to see Cannel and Brown looming over them both. "You're holding the only material witness to this investigation in your arms. She's coming with us."

"That makes you a lying bastard." Trying not to jostle Marybelle too much, Cam got to his feet. "I've got her, I rescued her, just like we agreed, and I'm taking her home to her son."

"I told you," Cannel was back to his smug self. "I would disavow all knowledge of you the moment you came into this compound, which means you're trespassing on a council investigation. This woman is the only remaining member of the fold left alive and she's coming with us. Hand her over or you'll be arrested and won't be tasting your mate's honey muffins for quite some time."

Cam snarled as he scanned the area, looking for an out. The guards were still at the gate, and he wouldn't be able to run far with Marybelle in his arms. Shifting was out of the question, but there was no way he was going to let the council get their hands on Fergus's momma. His ears picked up an unusual sound. Like wings flapping – big wings. Looking up, his snarl turned into a smile as a giant purple dragon circled then dropped into the compound with a thud. The flop of black hair hanging between the dragon's ears told him exactly who the lovely beast was.

"Do you want to say that again?" Cam asked. The ground shook beneath his feet as the dragon stomped over. "Do you want to explain to my mate that you're arresting me for saving his momma who you plan to interrogate when she's been gravely injured. Do you want to tell the one man who gave you all the information you needed to break the slavery ring and the plot against shifters everywhere that you're going back on your word to me?" He pointed at Fergus who had large smoke rings coming out from his long nose. "Tell him. Go on. Or I will, shall I?"

"Leave. My. Mate. And. Momma. Alone." Every word was punctuated with well-placed flames. Cannel and Brown jumped back as the grass they were standing on scorched black.

"You can't keep relying on your damn dragon to save you," Cannel yelled. "It's an offence to threaten council guards."

"Then stop threatening us." Cam caught the eye of the man he used to work with years before. "You there, can you help? I'm sorry, I don't remember your name right now, but I know you to be a decent man from when we worked together. These men and I had an agreement. This lovely dragon is responsible for the intel that allowed this raid. This woman, who's badly hurt and needs medical attention is his momma. That guard," he pointed at Cannel, "promised us that if Fergus told him all he knew, then no one would bother us anymore. Can I count on you to make sure that promise is kept?"

"I'm jealous as fuck you found your mate, man, and pleased as fuck you remembered your training or things could've gotten right messy with trying to apprehend the fold leader. Dead is the only result for scumbags like him, and without your cues, it wouldn't have happened." The guard nodded. "Catch your ride. I'll make sure you won't hear from us again in a professional capacity, on my wolf so be it."

"I appreciate that, I truly do. Look me up in Arrowtown

sometime if you're ever in the area. I run the local bar, and my mate runs the bakery, you'll always be welcome." Cam turned and eyed the impressive looking dragon. "Your momma needs the doc really quick, Fergus. Can you get us there?"

The dragon bent his long neck, sniffing at his momma. Marybelle's face was white, the strain showing in her eyes, but she reached up, a beautiful smile so like her son's gracing her face. "Hey baby," she murmured quietly as she stroked the side of his nose. "Your mate promised us honey muffins when we get home."

"Momma hurt." The deep guttural dragon tones were tinged with sadness.

"Not for much longer, baby. Just take us home and I'll be fine."

Cam couldn't identify the look his dragon was giving him, but he hoped, from the nudge he got on his shoulder, that they were going to be okay. Making sure Marybelle's coat was tucked around her as much as possible, he navigated Fergus's leg and found a spot to sit, with her still in his arms, on his dragon's back. *I didn't think I'd be doing this a week ago,* he thought as the magnificent animal took to the skies.

Chapter Twenty

Voices. Fergus could hear voices, but they were muted as though coming from far away. His body ached – his shoulders, his back, even his legs felt like something was pinning them down. He yawned, forcing his eyelids to work. Opening them, he found himself staring at Cam's worried face.

"I had the weirdest dream." Fergus managed a small smile, because seeing his mate's face was definitely something to smile about. "I dreamed I was a huge purple dragon, and I was flying so high in the night sky. And then I saw you…" Fergus's eyes widened. "Momma was hurt. People were dead all over the ground. Tell me. Tell me it was all a dream." He looked around, his breath quickening as he didn't recognize where he was.

"Babe, it's okay." Cam's hands cupping his face kept Fergus

grounded. "You did turn into a dragon. You saved me and your momma, baby. Don't you remember?"

Fergus thought hard – something difficult to do when his whole body felt as if he'd been hit by a truck. He remembered waking up... the note... "You left me," he cried, as everything came flooding back. "You didn't talk to me, tell me, nothing. You left me a note."

"And I would do exactly the same thing again in a heartbeat if it meant saving you from facing the bullies from your childhood." Cam's weight settled on the narrow bed Fergus was on. "Babe, you're at Doc and Joe's house. You managed to fly into town, landed on the main street and collapsed in a dead heap. You attracted quite a crowd."

Fergus rubbed his head. "I don't remember that bit. It

looks like I shifted though which was probably a good thing. I couldn't imagine shifting my bull form as a dead weight, let alone my dragon."

He looked up, meeting Cam's eyes squarely. "I understand why you did what you did, and I didn't doubt for a second you were supremely qualified for what went on. It's just, you made an assumption on how I'd react if you told me what you were going to do. The note said you expected me to be angry with you. You didn't give me a chance to show that might not have been the case. You made a major decision, one that affected both of us, without talking to me first and that hurts."

"Shit." Cam closed his eyes, his chin dropping to his chest. "I'd far rather anger you and have you yell at me, than hurt you any day. I'm so sorry. That was never my intention. I just wanted your momma to come home to you."

Fergus bit his lip. The bottom line was, his mate put his own life on the line to save the only woman Fergus had ever loved; the woman who'd shown him unconditional love every way she knew how, right down to pushing him out of the fold when his life was in danger. And their mating was so new.

Sliding his arms around Cam's neck, he pulled the man down and nuzzled his face against Cam's cheek. His mate's scent filled his nose, soothing him like nothing else could. Just inhaling his mate's uniqueness helped ease the aches in his body. He stroked Cam's head, just enjoying the closeness, as Cam's breath tickled his neck. "Did you mean it," he whispered, "in the note, I mean. Did 'love Cam' mean what it says?"

Cam nodded. "Every day since I met you."

Fergus tightened his arms around Cam's neck. "Next time you want to be romantic, take me to dinner first," he teased.

Cam snorted, and then he chuckled, his big body shaking. Fergus could feel all the tension in his mate's shoulders easing and he gave himself a mental head slap. His mate had been through a rough night, and probably hadn't had a wink of sleep. And that night, morning, whatever, wasn't over.

"Babe," Fergus said when Cam's chuckles died off, and the two men were just enjoying being in each other's arms. "You said momma had been hurt. How bad is it? Will she ever heal? What about my siblings – did the council find them? Give it to me straight."

After a long sigh, Cam pulled free of Fergus's arms and sat up, reaching for Fergus's hands and enclosing them in his own. "Your momma will live," he said gravely. "She had a mass of internal injuries and lost a lot of blood. Seth came in, you remember young Seth, the half-fae? Well, he came in, and healed as much as he could of your momma's insides, the bruises and the cuts on her face and she's breathing a lot better now. But Seth's healing can only work on what's there."

"Her legs?" Fergus remembered how they'd been covered when Cam was holding her back at the compound.

"The bastard sliced away some of her leg muscles, like he was hobbling her or some sick thing. Doc worked on her for over three hours, trying to piece some of the fragments back together, but in the end, she gave him permission to amputate."

Fergus gasped, his eyes filling with tears. "Both of them?"

Cam nodded. "One above the knee and one below about mid-calf. It was the only way. With all the damage she'd sustained, she couldn't shift and some of the injuries were at least a week old. Doc explained all of that to her, told her that with her legs damaged like they were, if he just patched her up it was unlikely she could ever shift. I'm sorry, I wanted to talk to you about that too, but you were still sleeping and so your momma asked me what I thought you'd want. I said, I told her that you'd just want her to smile again, and Doc said that was the best way to do it."

It was Fergus's turn to nod as he quelled his emotions, determined to focus on the future instead of what had been done to his loving momma. "Thank you. You did the right thing, said the right thing. I'm just sorry you had to..."

Cam stroked over Fergus's fingers, his cheeks red. "When I saw her, lying there back at the compound, covered in rags and stinking of blood. I told her who I was and why I was there, and do you know what she said?"

"What did she say?" It had to have been something special to make his military man blush.

"She said, now we were mated, that she was my momma too." Cam looked up and Fergus was startled to see his stoic mate was in tears. "I've never had a momma before. And now, now when I finally get one, I had to suggest she have her legs amputated." Cam was sobbing now, heaving gulps and masses of tears. "Life is so unfair. She never did anything in her life to deserve what was done to her."

"Hey, hey." Fergus pushed himself up, latching hold of his mate's shoulders, hugging him tight. "It's okay, it's all right.

You did the right thing. Momma would never be truly happy if she could never shift again. At least now she can, can't she?"

Cam's head nodded jerkily. "Doc gave her a light sedative, just after the operation was done. She was able to shift within half an hour and most of the surgical wounds are already healed."

"Then that's great news." Fergus hunted for his brightest smile and slapped it on. "And babe, if you haven't had a momma before, then you are in for a treat. Am I going to grill you endlessly about your life growing up at another time? You bet your sweet ass, I am. But when it came to handing out mommas, my momma is the best one anyone could have. You'll see. Now, we need to go and see her. Do I have any...?"

"You're not worried about your momma losing her legs, or my

part in it all?" The weight of Cam's body stopped Fergus getting out of bed, which was his intention. Fergus allowed it, because it was clear Cam was still struggling and he had to fix that first.

"She's still momma." Fergus struggled to find the right words. "Babe, she's alive and that's a huge blessing. If I know *our* momma, within a week, she'll either be organizing wheelchair races down main street, or running my bakery. I don't care which. But for decades, that woman had to pay a horrible price for giving her heart to the wrong asshole when she was young. But she always told me I was worth every tear. And this other shit, her life in the fold, losing her other kids – you watch. She will bounce back, and do you know why?"

Cam shook his head.

"Because the person who made me Fabulous Fergus was the Magnificent Marybelle and now she's free, she'll be even more amazing. Now, come on and move yourself. I need to dress, food would be nice, and then we're both going to see our momma with big smiles on our faces, right? No doom and gloom around momma."

"No doom and gloom." Cam still looked unsure, but he did move, after squeezing Fergus tight one more time. Fergus would work on his mate. When Cam got a full blast of Marybelle's magnificence, he'd understand.

Chapter Twenty-One

There was a tiny nagging voice in the back of Cam's head asking him if there was something wrong with his mate's ability to mentally process difficult situations. In the space of just two days, two days mind you, Fergus learned he could breathe fire when he got angry, turn into a big-assed purple dragon; he'd flown over two hundred miles on his first shift with passengers clinging to his back, and then woke up to find out his darling momma had lost both of her legs. That's without seeing the dead bodies of his ex-fold, coping with the hurt Cam had inflicted on him with his wretched note, and all the other upheaval that came from being a new mate. *Why wasn't he curled up in a heap in my arms crying his eyes out or angrily pacing and threatening to knock my head off?*

Watching Fergus chat happily with his momma, there was no sign of any breakdown. In fact, there was no sign of stress in his mate or his mate's momma. Marybelle was sitting upright in her bed, her hair combed nicely, and while her face was still pale, no one would ever guess she'd been a bleeding wreck of a prisoner less than twelve hours before.

Mrs. Hooper had apparently been over and introduced herself, producing a lovely night gown and a bundle of other clothes for Marybelle to wear. And now Fergus and Marybelle were discussing Mrs. Hooper's offer for Marybelle to stay with her for a while, until she got used to living in a shifter town.

"You could stay with me and Cam in my house, if you're not keen on being alone, momma. You don't have to go to Mrs. Hooper's." Fergus was sitting on the edge of Marybelle's bed, as bright eyed and gorgeous as he was any other day of the week.

"You and your fine hunk of a man are newly mated." Marybelle laughed and winked at Cam. "I can still see you through the day, but Mrs. Hooper has been very kind, offering to let me to stay in her home. It will be lovely, having another older woman around to talk to. She's a Texas Longhorn you know, so we're almost related."

"Mrs. Hooper's offer is lovely, momma, but I want to help you." Fergus was stroking his momma's hand. "I haven't seen you in so long. I'm worried..."

"You silly boy," Marybelle reached up, touching Fergus's jaw line. "You have nothing to worry about, not when it comes to me. I will be fine, and so will you. Now pay attention, we need to be serious for a minute."

Cam's animal went on alert. He'd been sitting in the corner of the room, trying to let Marybelle and Fergus have some time together, but being close enough to lend support if needed.

"What is it, momma? What did you need?" Fergus wasn't smiling anymore.

"I don't need anything," Marybelle said firmly. "You, my precious son, have done enough already. I know you've wanted me out of that fold for more years than we want to count, and I know how much I disappointed you, in not leaving sooner. But I made my choices based on what I thought was best at the time, and I will now live with the consequences of those choices."

Fergus looked as if he was going to argue, but Marybelle

held up her hand. "No, you need to hear this and this will be the last time we will be talking about it so make sure you listen carefully. I don't want you blaming yourself for what's happened to me or the fold members."

Cam frowned. *Is that what Fergus is doing? It doesn't show on his face.*

Marybelle wasn't finished. "I don't ever regret you being born; I don't regret pushing you out of the fold boundaries all those years ago, and I don't regret staying with the fold to keep you safe. I don't regret the two sweet boys I gave birth to after you were gone even if the circumstances of their conception is something I'd rather not think about. The thing is, Fergus my lovely, I know what you're like. You are going to see me getting around without my legs and find some way to blame yourself. It is not your fault."

"But…"

"No buts." Marybelle shook her head. "The day I held you in my arms for the first time was the happiest day of my existence, bar none. I have always seen you as the rainbow of my heart, the promise of a better life to come. And that promising future starts today. So, we will have no tears, no misguided guilt thinking you need to hover over me every five minutes, waiting on me hand and foot. I am going to stay with Mrs. Hooper and spend some time getting used to being away from the fold. I will grieve, in my own way, for the children I had, who never made it to school age, and then I will get on with forging a new life for myself."

"Can't I be a part of that life?" Cam tensed. For the first time since entering the room, Fergus sounded close to tears. "I've missed you for so long and the thought of not being near you now..."

"You will always be a huge part of my new life." Marybelle smiled and it was as wide and open as Fergus's usually was. "You and Cam are my beloved sons, but you are also grown men with lives of your own to lead. I know you built your bakery with me in mind and while we might have to lower the counter tops a bit, I will be in there before you know it, ordering you out, because you being with your mate is the most important thing in the world. I'm not leaving you. I'm never going to leave you again. But I must learn to stand, or sit, with my own two stumps, and Mrs. Hooper can help me with that. The best thing you can do to help me, is to be happy for me. Can you do that my Fabulous Fergus?"

Cam could see Fergus was struggling, could feel the tension now through their bond. But after a long minute, his wonderful mate straightened his shoulders and pasted on the biggest, and in Cam's opinion, fakest smile. "I am happy for you momma. I'm so happy you're here."

"And seeing your darling face means more to me than you can ever know. Now it's time for you to go." Marybelle laid back on her pillows. She did look tired. "Mrs. Hooper will be here shortly with my dinner and I doubt she made enough for you two. After that, her sons are going to help move me to her house so the good doc can have his bed back. You two need to get off home. You can come and visit tomorrow, after you've rested and taken care of yourselves. Have either of you even thought about the bakery or the bar today?"

"We have been a little bit busy, and Fergus was asleep for most of the day," Cam said as he stood up. Walking over, he rested his hand on Fergus's shoulder. "But the townspeople are very good at covering during a family crisis. I know you'll be very happy here, Ma... momma, and you know everyone including us, will help all we can. Come on, babe, let momma rest."

Fergus was torn – Cam could feel it in the sudden tension in his shoulders. But Marybelle tilted her head slightly, the shake so tiny it was easily missed. Fergus's nod was just as minute, and Cam wondered at the strength of their bond after so long apart. His smile still so fake it reeked of plastic, Fergus leaned over, kissing his momma on the cheek and patting her hand. When he stood and moved out of the way, Cam did the same, feeling a bit self-conscious when he did it, but it was worth it to see Marybelle's smile.

"Have fun you two." Marybelle waved and she was still smiling as they left the room.

Cam kept his concerns to himself until they got outside. Doc's surgery was only two doors down from the bar, so the walk to Fergus's house was short. But as they ambled along, hand in hand, the change in Fergus, the way his smile was now a lot more natural meant Cam just had to ask. "Don't you and your momma ever let anything faze you? Get you down? Upset you?"

Fergus scrunched his face. "What would be the point in carrying all that negativity?"

"Negative emotions are just as valid as positive ones," Cam huffed. "You don't have any issue showing when you're happy, and even on the odd occasion when you're sad. But why is anger, despair, and frustration an issue for you."

Fergus grinned as he looked up. "I thought sad and despair were the same things."

"You know what I'm talking about and to me, they aren't. Sad is something that happens when your pet dies. Despair is thinking you'll never own a pet again."

"I don't have a pet," Fergus said easily, swinging their joined hands as they walked along. "With my hours, and yours, it would be impossible to keep a pet happy."

"Fergus! You're deliberately misunderstanding my point." Cam stopped walking, spinning his mate around so they were facing each other. "Don't you ever let anything bother you? Show some anger, stamp your feet or throw something at a wall?"

"I don't mean to tease you. I do understand you're worried about me, but you shouldn't be." Fergus's hand was warm where it rested on Cam's chest. "I've never seen the point in hanging on to negative emotions. They weigh you down, and when they do that, they tarnish every aspect of your life, every decision, every interaction. Who would choose to live like that?"

Cam had a strong feeling Fergus wasn't understanding the point he was trying to make. "I know I don't have to tell you that life isn't always easy – I've seen and heard some of the shit you've been through. But babe, getting frustrated, or angry is a natural part of life. It's okay to show it especially in front of someone you trust, like your mate."

"And I do trust you. But the last time I expressed that anger, Brown almost lost his clothes. Babe, what would you have me do? I am pissed beyond comprehension at what's happened to my momma. The sight of those dead fold members, some of whom I was related to don't forget, will haunt me for a long time, and I could cheerfully resurrect that fold leader just so I could stomp on his head until it looked like a pile of cow dung."

That's more like it. Cam nodded to show he was listening.

"I had a long time to think when I was flying, and don't think I haven't been angry about my absent father and his flashy genetics on occasion too, especially recently. He could have at least tried to find me after all these years, and he never bothered. But what does me being angry do? What does it achieve?"

Cam had to think for a minute. "It would show the people around you, that you were understandably affected by what happened to you and momma," he said cautiously.

"But what would that achieve?" Fergus persisted. "Being angry in the moment is perfectly understandable, and in case you missed it, my dragon was angry you'd gone to the fold without us, and even doubly pissed off at those damn council guards who tried to arrest you again. But we're home now. The fold leader is dead, and yes unfortunately, so is the rest of the fold, but I can't do anything about that. Momma is here, wanting to live with Mrs. Hooper which I'm not sure about, but I'm just glad she's alive and well enough to make that decision for herself. You're here, safe, giving me a lecture in the middle of the footpath, and while I'd rather you kissed me, and held onto me as though I was someone precious, I understand you have anger you need to express, so I'm letting you talk to me like this in the hopes you'll let it go when you're done."

Cam wasn't sure he'd heard his mate correctly. "You're *letting me* express my anger, so I'll let it go?"

Fergus showed his teeth and nodded. "Giving you an outlet. You see, someone like me, who's had years of experience in shaking off negativity, can do it by acknowledging it, knowing I can't do anything about the circumstances, and letting them go. It's a subconscious thing, but it works for me. You're not wired the same way. You cling onto your emotions, holding them tight to your chest, so you need some way to ease that tension. Talking helps. Getting naked and pounding me into the mattress would probably be better, but we're standing on the footpath."

"You can't just shake things off." Cam's voice rose, even as the thought of pounding Fergus's butt made his cock tingle. "People died. I almost got arrested. You flew, for fuck's sake. Your momma lost her legs today. She'll never walk again!"

"I know." Fergus looked so impossibly calm Cam wanted to shake him. "But what can I do about any of those things? Will being angry raise the fold members from the dead? Will ranting about how unfair life is, bring momma back her legs, or grant her the ability to walk?"

"Well, no." Cam had a suspicion he was the one missing something now, but he didn't know what it was.

"Then there's no point in me hanging onto my anger about it." Fergus shrugged and then sighed. "Imagine this. Let's say I was hanging onto my anger about momma's situation, and Rocky came into the bakery complaining because I had sold out of eclairs, which he does at least once a day. Instead of feeling pride, or joy, because Rocky loves my baking so much, and teasing him about him having to find another excuse to escape Mal in twenty minutes so he can test a fresh batch, I'd probably snap at him, or worse. What if I started yelling at him for being so selfish because all he ever cared about was his eclair obsession? What if I told him how fat he was getting and how I had far too much to do to be worried about the eclair needs of one wolf?"

Cam had seen Rocky eat. It wouldn't be any more than the wolf deserved. But Fergus wasn't finished.

"He'd storm out and I'd probably lose a customer. By getting angry at Rocky, my mood would get worse and I'd probably snap at a lot of other customers too. Later, I'd close the shop and come down to the bar, and instead of smiling at you, I'd snap at you and probably refuse to even kiss you hello. I'd be grumpy and snarl at anyone who got close to me, and I'd be getting more tired too, because anger is a heavy emotion to carry around. So, my mood would get even worse again and by the time you and I got home, we wouldn't be speaking to each other, because my bad mood would make you grumpy too."

"It wouldn't."

"It most definitely would," Fergus said. "And I'd end up with your grumpy mood on top of my anger at my momma's lack of legs. So, we'd spend the night, not talking, not loving on each other. I'd get a lousy night's sleep, so by the time I got to the bakery the following morning, I'd barely be able to function. I'd still be in a shitty mood, to the point I would probably yell at Sensational Sarah. Then she would cry, and probably quit her job, then customers would be angry with me because I couldn't serve and bake at the same time, and in the meantime, you and I are still at odds, so I am feeling heartsick too, which means I'd be yelling at everyone and anyone and what does that achieve? Nothing at all, except the ruination of my business, the negative impact on yours and worse, a rift between you and I which would be excruciating. And that's all without factoring momma into the equation."

"What's momma got to do with all this?" Cam was still trying to make sense of the fiasco Fergus had described with

Rocky and its subsequent knock on effect with other customers, and their relationship.

"You said it yourself. She's got no legs, so every time I see her, I'm going to be reminded of what went down in that compound. And remember, I'm hanging onto my anger, tightly like a security blanket to the point I can't feel anything else. So, every day I see momma that festering anger mass is going to get bigger, to the point my mood is ugly every single day. I won't be able to talk to someone without complaining. I'd miss the beauty of my gorgeous tree in the back yard, because in my anger I wouldn't even notice it. Instead of celebrating my momma's life, and the fact I have a wonderful mate who loves me, I'd be bitter and horrible, and no one would want to be around me anymore." Fergus huffed.

"That's what anger does to people. The anger consumes them so much, they forget to look for the positives that could make them smile."

"I don't think you'd be that bad," Cam said, not quite sure how he'd lost control of the conversation.

"Anyone can behave that badly, including me." Taking a step closer, Fergus rested his head on Cam's chest. His voice was slightly muffled, but Cam could still hear him. "Anger is a choice, don't you see? Yes, some anger stems from deep-felt pain so bad it just has no other way of coming out, but ultimately, how we react to any situation at all is a personal choice. The anger doesn't happen to us, take us over and render us useless for anything else – a person chooses to take their anger out on others."

"Anger can sometimes be a good thing," Cam said, thinking

of some of his military situations where anger was the only thing that had kept him alive.

"I'm sure you've had more experience with that, than I have," Fergus agreed. "But anger isn't sustainable, just like hate. If those two emotions are clung to, they blind a person to the good in the world. You know, the person I'm ultimately angry with is the fold leader. If he'd been a decent man, then momma would likely still have her legs and she wouldn't be grieving for the loss of my two half-brothers, or the rest of her family. But he's dead. My anger won't touch him now, so there's no point in it. I'm making a conscious decision to let it go, following my lovely momma's example."

Cam couldn't help scoffing even as his arms slid around Fergus's back. "You'll be telling me next you forgive him or some such shit. The man was a monster. He could die a thousand terrible deaths and that wouldn't make up for all the harm he's caused."

"There's not a lot of point in forgiving a dead man either." Fergus chuckled. "When people say they forgive someone, that is their way of acknowledging their hurt and anger, and letting those negative emotions go. Some people find that process comforting, and it allows them to move past a tragedy and go forward with their lives. That's what momma and I have chosen to do – move forward with our lives."

"And what about me and the anger you claim I'm carrying?" Cam deliberately rolled his hips into Fergus's, loving the way Fergus's cheeks flushed red. "You said yourself I hang onto my emotions tight. What do you recommend for me?"

Fergus's head came up. "You start by smiling," he said with a cheeky grin.

"Like this?" Cam stretched his mouth muscles into a grin, or it might have been a grimace, he wasn't sure.

"More like this." Fergus's fingers tugged at the corner of Cam's lips, trying to force them upwards. "There you go."

"Really?" Cam worried his cheek muscles were going to crack. "Then what do I do?"

"Okay, you have tight shoulders." Fergus leaned back and eyed him critically. "Probably comes from maintaining your macho image all the time. You have to shake them out." He dropped his arms by his side and did an upper body shimmy. "Like this."

"You do realize we're still standing on the footpath, don't you?" *You do realize every rock of your body is rubbing on my dick.*

"You were the one who wanted this chat before we got home. Now shake your shoulders out, like I did."

Cam tried moving his shoulders in the same way as Fergus demonstrated. It didn't work because his arms were still resting behind Fergus's back.

"No, no, no." Fergus stepped back, which meant Cam's arms dropped. "Imagine moving like the agitator in one of those old washing machines. Shake your arms and shoulders out."

He demonstrated again, but as they weren't standing together anymore, Cam was now distracted by the sway of Fergus's hips. "Maybe you should show me more of these techniques at home." *Without clothes blocking my view.*

"Nope." Fergus shook his head. "We do it now. Otherwise,

you're going to carry that anger into our house, where it will seep into the walls and ruin the positive vibes our lovely home has got."

"We'll go into the back yard. I won't step foot in the house until we're done."

"We do it now. Shake babe. Shake the stresses out of those hunky shoulders of yours."

Which is how, Cam, reclusive and slightly arrogantly aloof bar owner and all round badass, found himself shaking his body, in the middle of the footpath, a block from their home. And of course, when the neighborhood children thought he and Fergus were dancing, they had to join in too. *The things I do to see Fergus smile.*

Chapter Twenty-Two

Someone is in our house. As soon as Cam was aware of it, he heard Fergus squeak and then seem to slump beside him. The dark room told him it was still the middle of the freaking night and someone was doing a piss poor job of trying to get Fergus off the bed. *Intruders,* Cam's honey badger snarled. *Intruders after our mate.* Fucking Cannel and Brown – Cam could smell them. Without second guessing his actions, he let his animal side take over.

Shaking out his fur, Cam whipped around and snarled. He was bigger than the natural form of his kind, a lot bigger. Brown and Cannel, they had Fergus's limp body between them and seemed to be doing their best to melt into the wall.

"Back off, Cam." Cannel put his hand out as though that would stop him. "I mean it. Back off now, or the bull shifting dragon will get hurt."

Stupid fucking council guards. Cam took two steps to the side of the bed, his mouth open, showing all his teeth. Fergus's torso was being hugged close to Cannel's chest, his mate's arms limp, his face slack. Brown had hold of Fergus's feet, his arms wrapped around his mate's calves as though that would save him. Cam braced his feet against the mattress and Brown yelled.

"We're going to bring him back. We won't be long. It's only a short acting drug. He has to talk, for our report. He has to..."

Cam heard 'drug' and didn't care about anything else. Launching himself off the bed, he snapped at Brown's legs first, catching the denim of the man's jeans in his teeth, the ripping caused as Cam's feet hit the ground. He roared then, a rattle roar, known only to his kind, furious at not hitting his mark. Cannel, left to handle Fergus's dead weight on his own, was moving towards the door, and yes, wolves could move faster than honey badgers on open ground, but a honey badger could speed over short distances if necessary. And as far as Cam was concerned, protecting Fergus came under the 'necessary' heading.

He baled the man up, in the corner of the room, his tail down, his four feet planted firmly on the carpet. He couldn't attack Cannel, who was wearing Fergus's body as a frontal shield. *Not yet, anyway.*

"You don't want to do anything stupid, Cam." Cannel's eyes were wide as he cowered back. But Cam could hear the rustle of clothes behind him and knew Brown was creeping up on him. He took another two steps closer towards Cannel, and as the whisper of air behind him moved, he did too – bunting his stout nose under Fergus's knees, lunging for Cannel's waist.

In his panic, Cannel threw Fergus aside, which was exactly Cam's intention. With Brown coming over him from the back, and Cannel blindly hitting out at his front, Cam turned to one side, snapping and snarling, tearing any flesh he could reach between the two men, his loose skin allowing him to twist out of any hands that managed to hold him, his claws making mincemeat of any skin that fell under them.

The pair were disorientated, many of their hits landing on each other instead of Cam. One of them, Cannel by the smell of him, landed on his back, trying a choke hold around his neck, but Cam shook, and his skin slipped and as Cam's shifted head was a lot smaller than the bulk of his body, he twisted out easily. The scent of blood filled the air, and with Fergus still sprawled on the floor by the door, Cam was incensed. As soon as he was free, he turned and attacked again – up on two legs, using claws and teeth; even his scent glands came into play at one point, filling the room with a foul stench that was going to be difficult to clean out.

"Wait. Wait." Brown backed off, gasping as he slid down the wall. Cannel was already lying on his side, groaning and clutching at a large scratch in his belly. "Shift man. For fuck's sake, shift. Let's talk about this like adults."

Cam grunted, backing up so his body was between the council guards and his mate. He just stood there, glaring, his lips still up, showing his teeth, his back ramrod straight. He felt his posture said all he had to say.

"Fine man, don't shift." Brown ran his hands through his hair. It came away bloody. "Look, you have to understand, you and that fucking dragon of yours have made us look seriously bad with the higher ups. Gower had no right to promise we'd leave you alone, not after the shit you pulled."

Gower. Now Cam remembered the name of the familiar face. *Good man. I owe him a drink or three.*

"Innocents died, man, don't you get it? Women and children, not to mention every man in that fold. They all died. Someone has to answer for that."

Cam didn't move. The fold leader and the council guards were responsible for the deaths. He and Fergus had nothing to do with any of it.

"Gods, you're a pain in the ass in that form, do you know that? I'm not going to be able to get the stench out of my nose for a month."

You're still talking. Count that as a win.

"The fact is, your mate and his mother are the only two people alive from that fold." Cannel had managed to right himself, although he kept a torn piece of his shirt over his nose, muffling his words. "They need to be available to talk to the higher ups about all they know."

Cam shook his head very slowly and deliberately.

"You can't hide them both forever," Brown yelled. "We're being investigated now. Three of our men died as well. They're making out we're incompetent, that we didn't factor in the leader chipping all his members."

Ooh. Cam wasn't going to let that go unchallenged. Shifting back to his human form in the space of a blink, he snarled with human teeth this time, his nudity not bothering him, although the stink his animal half left behind did – not that he'd let that show. "You *didn't* factor that in, even though you were warned about it. You went in, all guns blazing – shit, I heard the gunfire start before I'd even got over the wall. Instead of sneaking in, catching the leader unaware, making sure he didn't have access to that damn tablet you were waving about like a trophy, you dropped the ball. Those deaths are on your head and Fergus and Marybelle had nothing to do with any of it."

"We have to have something to show for…"

"You have got something." Cam flexed his biceps as he crossed his arms over his chest. "You've got a tablet, you've got the chips, you've got solid proof nearly all of those innocent deaths weren't caused by council guards. You've probably got records, sales of shifter children and the marks they went to. You've got enough to keep you going for a dozen lifetimes ironing out this mess."

"Nearly all of those innocent deaths?" Brown looked puzzled.

"The guards on the raid were trigger happy. Expect to get reprimanded for that. Out of all the guards I saw by the front gate, only Gower had any experience at all. He actually looked like he knew what he was doing. You wanted a showy arrest – live bodies to drag in front of the council so they can pin a medal on your chest. Well, shit happens. Thanks to your stupidity dozens of innocents died. Man up and take responsibility."

"You were there," Cannel's eyes narrowed. "We could take you in and question you all we damn well like. It's not like your dragon will stop us this time."

"Try it. In fact, go for it. I'm more than happy to stand in front of your superiors and tell them what I know. How you knew about the chips the fold leader was using but didn't take the warnings that the fold members might have them implanted seriously. How guns were fired before anyone got to the leader's house. How the guards chosen for the raid were still wet behind their ears and probably shot at the first thing that moved. How you tried to take an innocent woman, who had been a prisoner for god knows how long, into custody, for questioning when she'd been severely injured, something else you completely ignored. How you sneaked into my house, DRUGGED my mate and tried to take him by force, because you're too chicken livered to face his shifted form."

Cam lowered his voice as Fergus stirred. At least one thing the guards had said was true and the drug did appear to be short acting. "I'll tell them all that and more. And do you know what else I will do? When I've told informed the council of your incompetence, explained every single detail of what you did wrong, I'll make more calls and start talking to my friends in high places as well. I might be known in your circles as a fucking assassin, but I've spent a century making solid connections with people that matter. There's not a higher up in the military, or the shifter and paranormal councils who doesn't owe me a favor. Imagine what's going to happen to your careers when I start talking. You're lucky I shifted when you stole in here. If I'd stayed in this form, you'd both have broken necks. As it is, you're only breathing because the taste of human flesh gives my animal side gas."

Brown gagged and even Cannel's face went green. Cam sneered. "Yeah, I've done a lot of things in my life, not all of which I'm proud of. But I've never hurt an innocent and I'll be damned if I let any get hurt now. This is your final warning. Come near this town again, and you'll be dead. Come within a hundred yards of my mate or his mother again and I'll rip your throat out before you open your mouth. Now get out. Now!"

Brown pushed himself slowly to his feet. Cannel was having more trouble. "I'm injured man. Haven't you got a doc somewhere around here?"

Stalking over, Cam reached down, grabbed Cannel under one armpit and hauled him to his feet. The man immediately tried to hunch over, protecting his gut. "The doc's sleeping, much like everyone else in this town. He's tired because he spent hours trying to save Marybelle's legs, something he couldn't do due to the extent of the injuries you ignored. Performing two amputations is a lengthy process and he needs his sleep. Now, unless you want me to start amputating your body from the neck down, move yourself. You can crawl your way out of town for all I care."

Cam watched, waited, listened intently until he heard the front door slam and the sound of a car starting up. Only when he was sure the assholes had gone, did he consider the mess in the bedroom, and the prone body of his mate. Fergus's eyes were open, and his mouth was moving as if he was trying to speak.

Kneeling down by Fergus's head, Cam lifted it, resting it on his knee. "How are you feeling?"

Fergus tried to swallow. "You're naked." He grimaced and wrinkled his nose. "It stinks in here."

"I know, babe, and I'm sorry. Let's get you to my place for the rest of tonight. I'll arrange a clean up here for the morning."

Fergus looked as though he had a lot more to say, but he just moved his head – that was a sort of nod, and Cam would take it. Ignoring his need for clothes, Cam scooped Fergus into his arms, and headed out of the bedroom. *Maybe I should have left a window open,* he thought as he took his precious mate out of the house and started striding down the road. *If Rocky or Mal are on duty tonight, I'm going to have a lot of explaining to do,* he thought with a sigh.

Chapter Twenty-Three

On the surface of things, life was good. Well, it had definitely settled down, but as Fergus wandered into his bakery, giving a smile to Sarah who was taking another custom cake order, nodding to Brutus as he went through to the kitchen to find his apron, Fergus knew something was niggling him. He just couldn't work out what it was.

It'd been three weeks since momma had been rescued and Fergus had woken up after being drugged to find his house had been trashed – or at least his bedroom. The way the townspeople rallied around, cleaning, relining the bedroom walls, taking out the trash and installing fresh carpet was incredible. Cam bought all new bedroom furniture for them both, claiming it was his fault the mess occurred in the first place. Fergus didn't argue against the sweet gesture.

Marybelle was thriving, which did a lot to settle Fergus's mind. It was wonderful, being able to see her every day instead of waiting on once a week phone calls. Although, Marybelle was proving to be a busy lady. Having settled in with Mrs. Hooper, she learned how to get around in her new wheelchair within two days. Her face regained its round softness Fergus remembered from when he was younger, and she laughed so often, finding joy in everyone around her. Between helping at Mrs. Hooper's store and working with Sarah in the bakery, she never sat still and seemed to love and care for everyone in Arrowtown.

On the home front, he and Cam had settled into a new and comfortable routine. Brutus said he was more than happy to do the early morning starts at the bakery, and Nicky had now taken over the evening shifts at the bar full time. This meant the new mates could spend more quality time together, something Fergus adored. Cam was naturally reserved in nature, but he could be sweet too. Such as the time when one afternoon Fergus found Cam at home, under their big tree, with a beautiful picnic laid out for them to enjoy. They went to bed together at the same time every night, nearly always falling asleep wrapped around each other after a sensuous session. Sunday mornings were now spent in bed, watching movies, making out, and generally relaxing with each other.

Life was good, really good, which was why Fergus didn't understand why he wasn't feeling as settled as he should be. Slipping the apron over his head, he tied it behind his back and turned to see Brutus looking at him expectantly. "Try this," the bear said, holding out a muffin. "It's a new recipe I've been testing at home. Well, I found it on the internet, but it had bacon in it, and I thought why not give it a try."

"A bacon muffin?" Fergus took it and sniffed at it. "It smells delicious. What else is in it?"

"It's a pretty standard muffin mix, actually," Brutus said with a shy duck of his head. He was never very good at taking compliments, even for his baking. "It's also got natural yoghurt, bananas and seventy-five grams of grated cheese. I thought, seeing as most predators love bacon with anything, these could be a hit if you wanted to trial them out."

"I take it these have the Rocky seal of approval." Fergus grinned. "I also love how you think of recipes based on different shifter types. Like those kale and apple cupcakes you made last week. They just flew out the door once Sarah let her family know about them."

"Cakes can't be all about strawberries and chocolate." Brutus shrugged. "It's nice to have a variety sometimes."

"That's very true. I'll box up some of these to add to the pub lunch order today and we'll see what they say." Fergus took a big bite. Brutus had a light touch with his baking – the muffin was still slightly warm, with a fluffiness that hit Fergus's taste buds, making them sing. "Yum," he said as he swallowed. The balance of the sweetness of the bananas contrasted perfectly with the savory bacon, the whole thing evened out with the cheese and yogurt.

"That is... Oh, my gods." Slapping his hand over his mouth, Fergus ran out the back door to the small toilet attached to his shop. He'd barely made it when the delicious mouthful, and half of his undigested breakfast made an appearance. Still bent over, Fergus panted heavily through his nose, trying to quell the retching motions currently ruling his insides. "Well, that was unexpected," he said to himself as he managed to stand upright again. "I wonder..."

"Are you all right. Oh, my goodness, Fergus, say something." Looking over his shoulder, Fergus saw Sarah and an equally distraught Brutus watching him from the doorway.

"I'll be fine. I am fine." Reaching over, Fergus flushed the toilet, grateful he hadn't made more of a mess.

"Honestly, it's probably just something I ate."

"I swear I was careful with the ingredients." Brutus was wringing his hands looking as though he was going to cry. "Rocky's had a dozen of them or more, and Mal, Seth, Ra, Darwin and Simon too. Even the kiddies had some. That's why I was making them here. There was never enough of them left at home to bring in for you to try. I'm so sorry."

"It wasn't your muffins." Fergus leaned against the sink, running the cold tap so he could wash his face and hands. "The muffins were delicious," he scrubbed his hands, then sluiced his face, letting some of the water run into his mouth. His tongue felt decidedly furry. *I wish I had a toothbrush.*

Reaching for a towel, Fergus quickly dried himself off. Sarah and Brutus were still looking worried. "I'm sure it's nothing.

Maybe, the banana bacon combo reacted with something I ate for breakfast. Look at me. I'm fine, and Brutus your muffins were divine. We'll definitely trial them here.

"Now Sarah sweetie," he added, seeing as neither of his friends had moved from the door. "I need you to run across to Mrs. Hooper's and grab me a toothbrush and paste. One of those travel kit things will do. Brutus, I want another two dozen of those muffins made before the lunch order for the pub is due. Cam gets a lot of predators in that bar of his, and they are going to go nuts for anything with bacon in them. Move it, come on. We've still got a shop to run."

They left, but not without a lot of anxious looking back from Sarah, and Brutus looked like he wanted to shoot himself. Fergus checked his reflection. "I am perfectly fine," he told himself. "Hungry now, but per-fect-ly fine."

/~/~/~/~/

But Fergus wasn't fine. He managed to get through the rest of the day without any further incidents, and Cam loved on him just as he always did that night, never suspecting anything was wrong. But the next morning, Fergus gagged just walking into the bakery, and it seemed his stomach wouldn't settle until he'd thrown up. The third morning he didn't have breakfast, hoping that would help, but around ten o'clock he felt so woozy lifting a tray of eclairs from the oven, he dropped them. He made some toast, just plain bread and a hint of butter, and spent ten minutes hovering over the toilet bowl again.

"You have to see the doctor." Poor Sarah was so upset.

"What does Cam say about all this?"

"Cam doesn't know and you're not going to tell him," Fergus warned. "It's probably nothing, just a residual effect from the drugs those council guards pumped into me a few weeks ago."

"That was over three weeks ago," Brutus said. "And doc cleared you from that the day after it happened."

"Yeah, well he also couldn't tell me what they injected me with either, so you never know." Fergus inhaled long and slow. He was worried, deathly worried that the drugs had impacted him somehow, or maybe it was because he had a duel animal spirit. Maybe it was the drugs duel animal spirit combination, he didn't know. But no matter how worried he was, that was no excuse to take it out on his friends.

"I'll pop in and see the doc after I've dropped off the lunch order for Cam, all right? But no breathing a word of this to anyone. The last thing a bakery needs is the reputation of being owned by someone who can't stop throwing up. We'd never get any sales. Go on, back to work. I've got to remake these eclairs."

Of course, sneaking into the doc's office, when it was just two doors down from Cam's office, wasn't going to be easy. Cam liked to watch him walk back up the road after the delivery, part of his protective nature. Fergus would get to the bakery, turn and wave. Cam would wave back and then they'd both get on with their day until Fergus closed up his shop. *I'll just have to come up with an excuse for him not to do it today. With any luck, he'll be busy and won't notice.*

Chapter Twenty-Four

"Hey, was that your Fergus I saw skulking into the doc's office?" Liam said cheerily as he sauntered into the bar. Since mating to his two hunks, and having a child, he'd cut down his hours as a deputy, preferring to spend time at home. But it was early afternoon, and he looked very handsome in his uniform. Taking off his hat, he rested it on the bar. "I'll just have a soda. It's as warm as hades out there today. So, how have you been keeping?"

"Good. Everything's good." Cam frowned as he reached down into the refrigerator and pulled out the soda Liam wanted. "What did you say about Fergus? He was just here. Wasn't he going back to the shop?"

Liam shrugged. "Not unless the bakery's moved. He was going into doc's as I came around the corner. Oh, my goodness, don't tell me he's delivering his baked goods around town now. Rocky will have him run off his feet delivering to the council offices all the time."

"The only place he delivers to is here." Cam thought back over their lunchtime visit. Fergus looked a little pale, but he didn't say anything about needing a doctor. Checking the bar, Cam saw no one but the regular crowd. "Keep an eye on this place for a minute, will you?" He asked Liam. "Sue's on her lunch break but she will be back in shortly. I'll just go and see if Fergus needs a hand with anything."

"A hand." Liam leered and wiggled his eye brows. "I know all about mated hands. I've got two of them myself, well, mates, I mean. Between them, they have four hands."

"Yeah, something like that." Cam wasn't going to disabuse

Liam of his assumption. "I won't be long." He jumped over the bar, heading for the door.

"Maybe that's part of your problem," Liam called out. "If it doesn't take long, you're not doing it right." A chorus of laughter followed Cam out of the door.

Ha, fucking ha, ha. Cam sprinted across the road, letting himself into the doc's hallway. The waiting room was on the right, the door wide open. The room was empty, but the door into Doc's office was closed. Cam debated for all of two seconds, before knocking on the door and opening it.

He peered round. Fergus was lying on the bed, his shirt off, looking even paler under Doc's bright lights. "Ah, Cam," Doc beamed. "I was wondering how long it would take for the gossips to tell you Fergus was here. I was just congratulating him. He's about a month into his pregnancy from what I can tell."

"Pregnant?" Cam almost fell into the door, righting himself long enough to make it to the side of the bed. "How? I mean why? I mean... what the fuck?" He fumbled for Fergus's hand, hanging onto it as though it was a lifeline.

"It was a bit of a shock to me too," Fergus said quietly. "I didn't think... I've been raised as a bull shifter all my life..."

"Yes, well Mother Nature will have her way, and it would seem your dragon genetics are stronger than most." Doc smiled and patted Fergus's other hand. "It's all very fascinating really. I mean, Seth was unusual being half fae half rabbit, but it was magic that allowed him to get pregnant and give birth. I've never heard of a half-breed shifter who has one furry and one non-furry side. From what you said, your dragon half only came out after Cam claimed you, is that right?"

Fergus nodded. "But I can still change into my bull side too. Cam and I both shifted to play in the garden last night and I was very definitely furry then."

"And you're very definitely pregnant now, so whether your dragon makes an appearance or not, he's definitely working well on your insides."

"I just never dreamed it was possible." Cam stroked the hand he was holding, studying Fergus's torso. It looked as slender as it always did. "I mean, we all know, we grow up knowing furry male shifters can't get pregnant. But a half dragon? Shit." Cam panicked as he thought about the ramifications. "Is Fergus's dragon half strong enough to carry the baby to term? Can he shift and if he does should it be into his bull or dragon form? What about the drugs he got stuck with a while ago? Have they hurt the baby in any way? How soon can you tell?"

Doc didn't seem fazed by Cam's questions. If anything, he seemed amused by it. "Believe me, when I got pregnant it was just as big of a shock. But as for the dragon being strong enough – Fergus, you wouldn't have gotten pregnant if the dragon inside you couldn't carry the baby to term. As for the drugs, they were out of your system a day after you got injected. It was a council made concoction so it should be safe for all shifters. They weren't trying to hurt you."

"No, just steal him away." Cam's heart leapt in his chest. *What if they'd succeeded. Fergus could be sitting now, in a council jail, not sure what was happening and probably pining for me. He could've been held for months. Once the council learned he was pregnant, there's no telling what they'd have forced him to admit to, just to save their own hides. My gods, and if they'd taken him, I'd probably be in the cell next to him, after trying to save him. I wouldn't be any help to him at all. What if...*

"Cam!" Cam was snapped out of his worry by Doc's harsh tone. The doc held up a wand-shaped instrument. "Thanks to the efforts of the fundraiser held in your bar, we can see what's going on inside of Fergus. Will that help?"

"It's either that, or you'll have to shake out your shoulder's again," Fergus teased. Cam was pleased to see he'd gained a bit of color in his cheeks.

"I'm not doing that in here." Once on the street was enough for Cam. "Thanks, doc, yes. I think we'd both want to see what's going on inside of my mate, and maybe then you'll have some idea of a time line. Before the birth, I mean." Even as he spoke, Cam was already running the numbers. Honey badgers in the wild were pregnant for about six months, or one hundred and eighty-one days. Scottish Highland bulls, in their natural state, had a longer gestation period – more like nine months, or up to two hundred and ninety days. A dragon on the other hand...

It seemed the doc had been thinking along the same lines. "From what I studied in college, and from the information I gleaned from on the paranormal website, dragons have a very short gestation period in comparison to other larger animals, only about three months." Doc had a tube and was running a line of lube across the base of Fergus's belly. "Dragon pregnancies are very rare. It's why I was surprised when Marybelle told me your sire left her, Fergus."

"He broke her heart, I know that." Fergus gasped as Doc pressed the wand on his belly. "But she never mentioned if her pregnancy was shorter than her others."

"We can ask her, if that helps." Cam was split between watching the doc, and watching the strange blobs moving around on the screen the wand was attached to. "How on earth are you meant to make anything out of those blobs?"

"It's all very easy when you know what to look for." Doc moved the wand and pressed around some more. "Ah, there we are. It's never an exact science, knowing where the womb is going to locate itself in a male shifter. But there we are."

"Womb?" Cam felt his knees wobble slightly and he straightened them. "Fergus has a womb?"

"Well, where else is a baby going to grow, numbnuts." Doc chuckled. "I suppose in your head, a cute little fetus was just floating around Fergus's other vital organs, snatching a bite to eat from whatever he could find."

"I know they don't do that." Cam's cheeks were fiery, he could feel them. "But if Fergus's dragon only manifested when I claimed him..."

"The dragon was always there," Doc said patiently. "That's why I'm surprised the sire was never around. Dragon spirits can lay dormant for centuries. If a male half-breed never takes a mate, then he could die, never knowing he had the potential to let his dragon out. In typical dragon half breed circumstances, the sire would arrange for a mating as soon as the child came of age, simply to force the dragon out of his slumber. It doesn't always work. A true mate is the only firm guarantee of a successful dragon wakening, but sometimes the bond bite of a strong male can trigger it."

"Well, let's just say I'm glad that never happened," Fergus said brightly as Cam growled. "What can you tell us of the lumps and bumps I see on the screen?"

"That you have a healthy, well-formed baby," Doc said, twisting so he could point to the screen with his free hand. "Spine, head, legs and arms. The child has fingers, toes, and facial features. The tail has completely been absorbed and from the size, I'd be guesstimating your little one is about twelve weeks, possibly fourteen weeks along, although

I will know more on the next scan. With shifter babies, it's not always to tell from just one scan."

"We've only been mated seven weeks – two months at the most. That means, that would mean..." Cam dropped Fergus's hand; his heart was beating so fast he couldn't hear anything for the rush of blood in his ears. *Oh, my gods, surely not...*

"Oh, Fates save me from clueless males." Doc banged his head on the bed. "The baby's yours, dimwit. I can tell by Fergus's scent and you could too if you just used your animal senses more often. I was using the human developmental framework because we know humans gestate for forty weeks. All shifters are different, especially when a couple is a mixed pair like you and Fergus."

"Okay." Cam would listen, but only because his heart refused to think anything else was possible. He went to take Fergus's hand again, only slightly mollified when Fergus allowed it although he didn't look his normal happy self.

"Look, it's basic biology. You have a dragon who gives birth in three to four months. Honey badgers are around six months. Scottish Highland shifters have the longest pregnancy out of the three of the genetics that make up this baby at roughly nine months. With this combination baby, what am I meant to do? Put all three time spans in a hat and pull out one and hope that's it?"

"All babies develop along the same lines?" Cam's heart rate settled down.

"Yes, even in cases like Simon's when he had his babies in shifted form. That's why I needed the ultrasound machine. By taking a base reading now, and another one in a week's time, I can see how much the fetus has grown and will have a better idea on when he or she will be born."

"Oh shit, the birth. How…"

"We'll worry about that next week," Doc said firmly, putting the wand in a holder and handing Fergus some tissues. "I'll leave you alone for a few minutes, Fergus. I believe Cam has some groveling to do, then I'll come back and we can talk diet, rest and exercise."

"Thanks, doc." Fergus cleaned up his stomach. Cam mentally whacked himself around the ears. *How could I even think…?*

/~/~/~/~/

I'm not dying of some mysterious illness. Those drugs aren't having an effect on me anymore, or the baby and now I know I'm just suffering from morning sickness. All ticks in the plus column. Fergus sat up, throwing the dirty tissues into the bin and reaching for his shirt. He felt surprisingly happy about the impending birth. Sure, it was a shock when the doc told him, but the ultrasound confirmed what the pee stick told him. *Now what to do about my clueless mate?*

Pulling his shirt over his head, Fergus asked, "Who told you I was at the doc's?"

"Liam." Cam sounded distracted. "He was worried you'd taken up a delivery service, Rocky would never get any work done if that was the case."

"Uh huh." Fergus swung his legs over the side of the bed but remained sitting on it. "I am guessing you realized after talking to doc I wasn't a slut before we met, I didn't trick you into claiming me, and that the baby is yours."

Where Cam's cheeks were red before, now his skin was pale.

"I wasn't thinking. I've never been in this position before. The words came out, and then the damage was done, and fuck, I don't know what to say now."

"Hmm, well good thinking that words have power and it's really hard to walk back something stupid when you've said it out loud. Maybe my influence is rubbing off on you at last."

"It is." Cam nodded, not looking at him. "It definitely is and it's a good influence too. A great influence, that you have on me I mean."

Fergus hated that his huge mate looked so unsure of himself. In every other situation Cam was a confident god who walked among mere mortals. It was touching that he felt he could be this vulnerable in front of Fergus, but it was totally unnecessary. Fergus had been hurt, but only for a moment. He'd been shocked when the doc had told him as well.

"I'm guessing, if in other matings one person put their foot in their mouth and said the wrong thing, the first thing the offender would say when they realized their mistake was that they were sorry."

"I am so sorry."

"And then, because we're in a doctor's office, and we have had some big life changing news, they would probably say something like, I'm really blank, blank, blank learning about the new baby, with you filling in the blanks of course."

"I'm thrilled. I'm stunned. I'm over the moon. I'm scared. I'm anxious. I'm worried. I'm happy, oh, my gods, I am so happy. I'm..."

"Just like a new dad would be hearing the news." Fergus reached out, pulling a willing

Cam closer so he could rest his head on his mate's stomach. "I'm all of those things too, but the main thing I feel is total confidence, because I've got you and I know nothing will ever harm our little one with you around."

"I won't let you down." Cam's arms rested on Fergus's shoulder and Fergus could feel fingers threading through his hair. "I won't let you or the little bump down. I'll make mistakes. I'm sure I will. I haven't got a clue about how to be a father. But I'm a fast learner."

Fergus looked up. "You never did tell me what happened to your parents."

"Because there was nothing to say." Cam's jaw set in a tight line. "I never knew my father. I remember my mother, vaguely. From the time I could walk I was often left on my own, and then one day she just never came back. I never heard from her again."

Oh no. Fergus rubbed up his mate's arms, offering him comfort. "How old were you when she left?"

"Nine, ten, something like that. Times were different back then. No one blinked an eyelid at a child alone. I guess she owned the house because no one kicked me out of it, but I lived alone until I looked big enough to join the army."

"How old were you then?"

"Fourteen, fifteen. Just after my first shift. I had a lot of catching up as far as schooling went. I'd never been to school and could barely read or write, but the guy who signed me up liked my size and I learned as I got on."

"Oh, babe." Fergus's heart melted for the young man Cam had been – so alone in the world with no one to hold him and let him know he was going to be okay. Fergus had been alone too, not much older than Cam had been, but he'd always known his momma loved him unconditionally. "Our child won't grow up alone."

"No, they won't." Fergus smiled as a touch of Cam's confidence showed in his voice.

"They'll be loved, cared for, taught how to cope with life's ups and downs," Fergus continued softly. "Safe in the knowledge their parents love each other forever more."

"I do you know." Cam nodded. "I love you so much sometimes I think my heart's going to burst with the wonder of it."

"I love you too." Fergus realized in that moment that was the first time he'd actually said the words. "I will always love you."

"And our little fig."

That wasn't a question, but Fergus nodded anyway. "Come on," he said, suddenly needing to get Cam alone and out of the doctor's office. "Let's call doc back in, find out how long I'm going to be allowed to have sex for, and then head home for the afternoon. I think this sort of news deserves a nap time."

"Nap time?" Cam hugged him close and then let him go.

"You know, naked in bed in the middle of the afternoon when everyone else is busy working – that sort of nap time."

"Ah," Cam smiled, looking almost giddy. "The non-sleep nap variety. I like it." He sobered up, leaning forward and dropping a kiss on Fergus's nose. "Congratulations, babe. I'm really truly happy I'm going to be a daddy."

"Congratulations to you too, babe. After all, you were part of this too." Although Fergus wished he hadn't mentioned that last part as for the next hour doc drilled them on everything from vitamins to sexual habits. What was worse was the number of pamphlets Cam left with, including a do's and don'ts list a mile long. *By the Fates I hope this baby takes after the dragon shifter's side.* Otherwise, it was going to be a very long pregnancy.

Chapter Twenty-Five

It was time, Cam could feel it in his bones. For the past three mornings he'd woken up in his animal form, his face resting against Fergus's baby bump. And it was a huge bump – five months in the making, during which time Fergus had smiled, joked about not seeing his feet and been the model of patience even when Cam tried to forbid him from working. In short, his mate had had an amazingly hassle-free pregnancy.

The same couldn't be said for Cam. He worried – a lot – about all sorts of things. Was the baby growing the way it should be, was Fergus getting enough rest? Was his diet nutritionally balanced enough to give their new baby the best start in life? What type of shifter would the baby be, or was his genetics such a pea soup of different animal types, would the baby even shift at all? And if the young one couldn't shift – what then? Would they be bullied and tormented in a shifter town, would he and Fergus have to move?

Fergus, bless his big and open soul, took all Cam's worries and let them go. Just pouf – gone – something Cam still couldn't work out how to do even after seven months of living with his mate's beaming smile. He remembered grumbling about it to Ra once, after a few too many whiskeys in the bar. But Ra wasn't any help either and he had three kids. He just said what would happen would happen, and there was nothing Cam could do about it until it did.

But now it was happening. Today was the day. Cam fretted even as his animal side sniffed along Fergus's baby bump and then licked it. The birth was going to be a csection. He and Doc had discussed it at length. Because Fergus was only half dragon, they couldn't trust his magical nature would come to the party on the day, so Doc wasn't taking any chances.

Which meant Cam had to call him as the Doc would need time to prepare. And that meant shifting and finding clothes because walking naked down their road once was enough. Mrs. Flaherty still winked at him, every time they passed in the street and Cam could only wonder what she was doing peering out of her curtains in the middle of the night.

The baby. His animal side was getting most insistent and willingly let Cam's body morph into his human side. Fergus was still sleeping – his full lips open slightly, gently snoring. But as Cam watched, Fergus flinched and his hands went to his belly, stroking it. When it happened for the second time, Cam moved.

Snatching the phone from the side of the bed, Cam hurried into the bathroom and closed the door. Pushing the number he had on speed dial, he was thankful when Doc answered after the second ring. "It's time," he said quickly, keeping his voice low. "My animal's screaming at me, and Fergus is flinching in his sleep and rubbing his belly."

"It matches the dates we had," Doc said brusquely. "Bring him in and don't forget a bag of clothes for the little one." He disconnected the call before Cam had a chance to ask anything else.

Think of this like a military operation, Cam told himself as he peed, then washed his face and hands. Operation bring baby home. The nursery was ready – Mrs. Hooper and

Marybelle being surprisingly helpful on what was needed. It seemed like everyone in town was holding out for the birth, offering gifts and suggestions in equal measure.

And now it's time. Going back into the bedroom, Cam silently got dressed, hunting for the bag Fergus had packed the week before. It was all ready. Cam couldn't help but pick out one of the little onesies Dave Hooper from the bar had bought for the baby. It was bright red, with a honey badger snarling on the front of it and the words "My dad's a badass, what's yours?" *Just one more little thing my mate does for me, choosing this as the baby's coming home outfit,* Cam thought fondly as he put it back in the bag again.

Okay. I'm ready. Cam strode out of the room. He was almost at the door when he stopped himself. *Damn idjit,* Cam slapped his head, dropping the bag and rushing back to the bedroom.

Fergus was awake, his eyes sleepy, his hand moving restlessly over his bump. "Did you forget something, mate of mine?"

"It's time, isn't it?" Cam came over and caressed Fergus's bump. "Our little one wants to see your smile."

"And feel your hugs," Fergus smiled, but it was tight. "Can we?"

"Going now." Cam found a pair of sweatpants, the only thing that fit Fergus anymore and gently eased them over his mate's legs. "Do you need to pee, or…"

"I don't think we have the time. I'm a little worried if our little fig doesn't get out soon, they're going to develop claws and cut their own way out." The fact that Fergus let his wince show, while awake, was telling.

"You're in pain." That went against everything Cam stood for. Whisking Fergus into his arms, he ran through the house, out the door, totally forgetting the bag, his boots pounding on the footpath.

"Cam. Babe. The bag." Fergus was trying to be reasonable; Cam knew that was just who his mate was, but there were tight lines around his mate's gorgeous mouth and eyes, and Cam wasn't going to allow that a second longer than necessary.

"Later." There was no way of knowing how long Fergus had been in labor. *For fuck's sake. I was sleeping. How the hell could I sleep at a time like this. I should've known... I should've...*

Deputy Joe was just coming out of the Doc's home as Cam ran up. "Leave it open.

Emergency coming through." Yes, he was yelling, but who the hell cared. Ignoring Joe's knowing smirk, at least the deputy left the door open, Cam barely noticed Joe tipping his hat to Fergus as Cam pushed them past him.

"Doc. Doc." Was Cam still yelling? It seemed he was, because he got a headshake from the man who was at least dressed in scrubs and looked professional enough.

"Put him on the bed, then wait outside."

"Outside! You've got to cut him now." Cam managed to be gentle placing Fergus on the bed, but he was ready to tear strips off Doc. "I have to be here."

"You will get outside, now. I'm not fighting your animal when he smells your mate's blood. I need to be focused on Fergus." Doc pointed at the door.

Cam was torn. Fergus was in pain. The baby needed to be born. But he couldn't let doc cut into him without being there. *A Komodo dragon. I can take him. No. No. No.* Now Cam was warring with his animal side. *We need the doc. But... but...* He whirled as hands gripped his biceps, while an arm wrapped around his neck. "What the hell?" Liam, Deputy Joe and Rocky were all hanging onto him and dragging him towards the door. "I've got too..."

"The Doc said out," Rocky grunted. "Good luck, Fergus. We'll make sure this one doesn't come to any harm."

"Love you, babe," Fergus called out cheerfully, and that was the last thing Cam saw as Mal of all people closed the door, blocking his view.

"You fucking assholes." Now Cam was mad. Twisting and kicking out, he tried to get free, but it was a lot harder in his human form. "You motherfucking pieces of shit. I'll get you for this. That's my mate in there. My baby."

"Right outside," Rocky ordered quietly, tightening his grip around Cam's neck. "We can't leave him in the waiting room like this. He'll scare women and children."

"You can't do this to me." The men had dragged Cam right out of the house, still kicking and yelling for all he was worth. On the street, Cam tried to get traction with his boots, but the damn shifters holding him were too strong.

"Pubs not open yet," Joe said cheerily. His hair was mussed, and he seemed to be limping slightly. "The alley might be a good place to sit on him, until Doc is done. Taking him to the diner isn't fair on anyone else."

"I'll do you, you fucking bastard." Cam would not give

up. "I thought you were my friends."

"We are your friends, numbnuts." Mal stepped in front of him, chin raised as if daring Cam to hit him. Which Cam might have done, if it wasn't for the fact that a bloody lion and a bull shifter were hanging onto his arms, and his neck was being squished by a cocky wolf. "Doc needs to focus. Fergus is a half-breed; he doesn't know what's going to happen when he cuts your mate open."

"That's why I need to be in there," Cam snarled.

"No. You don't." Rocky grunted as Cam threw some of his weight into his shoulders. "Your animal is a give no shit, take no prisoner, hard ass type. One whiff of blood, and there's no telling what you would do. Now settle the fuck down and be reasonable about this."

"Reasonable? What the fuck is reasonable about you guys ambushing me, in front of my mate?" Cam was panting so hard he could barely speak.

"I'm not allowing you to tear strips into my mate for doing his job." Joe grunted under the effort of holding him. "In ten minutes, this will be over, and you can see Fergus and the new baby. Ten minutes. You just need to calm down."

"I need to smash someone, and you're a handy target." Cam tried to do just that, but Liam was hanging off his other arm. "Fuck, you guys eat far too much of my mate's baking. At least let me get a punch in."

"I'm already going to have bruises," Liam snarled. "You'd better hope that baby of yours is cute, otherwise you're going to have a pissed off wolf and a phoenix after your ass."

"The baby. Fuck." All the fight went out of Cam like someone had flicked a switch. "The baby's coming... today... like in the next ten minutes. Oh, my gods, what if they look like me?"

"Finally." Cam felt the weight of Rocky's body against his back and the hold around his neck loosened. "The big guy finally gets it."

"You don't know the sex of the baby yet?" Mal asked, pulling up an old beer crate and sitting on it.

"Fergus wanted it to be a surprise." Cam shook off the holds on his arms and from around his neck, leaning against the wall rubbing his face. "I didn't care either way, but shit, what if the little tyke is like me?"

"Personally, I'm hoping for someone more like your mate," Rocky said. "We already have a good bar, but you can never have too many bakeries. I think there should be one on every street corner."

"That's only because then you wouldn't have to walk so far to get your fix," Mal teased, slapping his friend in the leg. "The walking is good for you, burns off all those extra calories."

"He won't let me use the patrol car to buy supplies," Rocky said mournfully. "He considers it a waste of resources."

Cam snorted and then laughed. It wasn't so much what Rocky said, but the puppy dog look on his face was hilarious. Mal must have been immune, because he just laughed too. And then Cam had a horrible thought. "Oh, no. I forgot the bag Fergus packed for the baby. It's still sitting just inside the front door of the house."

"Well," Joe said, grinning as he pulled out his phone, and glanced at the screen. "Now the danger to my mate has passed, I'll pop along and pick it up. I doubt you even thought to close the front door, running like a maniac down the street. Congratulations, daddy. You have a beautiful nine-pound five-ounce baby boy."

"I'm a dad. Oh, my fucking gods, I'm a dad, guys. Did you hear?" But Cam didn't wait for a response. He was running around Doc's house, bursting through the door.

Marybelle and Mrs. Hooper were hovering by Doc's surgery door, Marybelle moving her chair out of the way as soon as she saw him. "Everything went perfectly," she said with a huge smile. "Go in and meet your new son."

"How did you know?" Cam meant to call her. In fact, he distinctly remembered promising her that he would.

"You men," Mrs. Hooper scoffed. "Like anything would happen in this town without us knowing about it. You yelling your silly ass off all the way down the street was clue enough. Look at the state of you."

"I'm sorry." Suddenly Cam was conscious of how he looked, his shirt half out of his waistband and most of the buttons undone. Running a hand over his non-existent hair, he pulled down his shirt and tucked himself in. Inhaling sharply, he let the breath out slowly. "Excuse me, ladies. I need to see Fergus and my son."

Easing past the ladies, Cam felt as if he were walking into a dream. Fergus was upright on the bed, a gentle smile on his face, cradling a bundle against his naked chest. Even Doc looked up and gave him a smile before busy scribbling notes on a pad on the desk.

"He's here, babe. We did it."

The prickle of tears wasn't a usual feeling for Cam, but he

ignored them as he made his way to the side of the bed. Cupping a hand around the bundle, he searched Fergus's face for any sign of stress. "Are you okay," he asked softly.

"I've got stitches, but a couple of shifts should take care of that. Doc suggested I leave doing that for a day or so, just to let my body calm down first. It seems our son was in a bit of a hurry. Are you all right?"

"Perfect now. Gods, I love you so much." Cam leaned forward, brushing his mate's forehead, nose, and finally his lips with his own. "So very much."

"I love you too." Fergus jiggled the bundle in his arms slightly. "So, what do you think of our son? Here, you can take him."

You want me to hold him? But this wasn't Liam's child, or Joe's or Simon's or Ra's. *This is our son.* His heart in his mouth, Cam carefully eased the warm bundle out of Fergus's arms, bringing it up to his chest so he could see.

The features were squishy and chubby, the baby's eyes tightly closed although Cam noted long dark lashes. His nose was cute, with a slight turn up at the end, and there were wisps of black hair sticking up from his head. Cradling his son on one arm, Cam opened up the blanket, stroking a finger over the little barrel chest, his arms, and tiny fingers.

"He's amazing," Cam whispered just as his son's eyes flew open. Brilliant blue eyes latched onto his, and Cam knew he was in the presence of an old, *old* soul. *Possibly another dragon then.* "Hello, precious. I'm your other daddy. Welcome to Arrowtown."

The baby yawned, flung one of his arms around, and then closed his eyes again. Cam looked up to see the room full – Marybelle, and Mrs. Hooper,

Rocky and Mal leaning on each other, while Liam propped up a wall. Deputy Joe was there with his and Doc's two kids, and the forgotten bag. Sarah turned up, and Brutus, who was munching on what looked like a custard square. "I just heard," Brutus said, swallowing quickly. "I've got to get back. There're eclairs in the oven. Just wanted to say congratulations. I'll catch up with you later."

"You left eclairs in the oven to burn," Rocky yelled, running out after the bear. "You heathen. I'll..."

"And that's my cue to go too." Mal sketched a salute. "Huge congratulations, guys." He ran off after his friends.

One by one, people stopped to say hello, coo over the baby, and congratulate Fergus. It was an hour, maybe two before the doctor's surgery was quiet once more. Perched on the edge of the bed next to Fergus, Cam wasn't in a hurry to move. He didn't realize just how many friends he and Fergus had, but he was filled with a quiet sense of pride and belonging he'd never had before. But when the Doc checked Fergus's stitches, and told them they could go home, provided Fergus took things easy, Cam was ready. It was time for the hard work to begin. Their son might be sleeping now, but Cam could see the mountain of sleepless nights they would be getting through in their future. He couldn't be happier about it.

Epilogue

"Come on little Ivan, come and see the wonderful big outdoors," Fergus crooned to their son as he took him out into the back yard. Ivan was now five days old, and a placid baby for the most part. The only time he cried or made a fuss was when he wanted feeding, which seemed to be every two hours. Fergus had left Cam sleeping, the lure of the early morning quiet too sweet to ignore. The air was warm, and the sun was just peeking through the leaves as he stepped out onto the lawn.

"The world is such a beautiful place, sweet Ivan." Fergus kept his voice soft as he picked his way over the grass. "Full of birds and plants and animals and life. You just have to take the time to stop and appreciate it."

He stopped underneath the big tree that had drawn him to the house in the first place. "You see this." Stepping close to the tree trunk, he held Ivan's hand against the bark. "See how big and strong this tree is. You want to be like a tree, my precious darling, with deep roots and a strong core, just like your daddy has." He looked up at the leaves as Ivan murmured. "Me, I'm more like the leaves up there dancing in the wind. But see, I can do that, because your daddy is like the roots and the trunk that keeps me anchored."

Ivan squealed and waved his free hand about and Fergus laughed with him. "It is beautiful, isn't it darlin'. But come on, let me lay you down and then you can see what I love most about this tree."

Spreading out a blanket wasn't easy one handed, but Fergus got it opened enough for them both to be comfortable. Getting them both on the blanket, he cradled Ivan with one arm, pointing up with the other. "See there, all the shapes, all the clouds. Look how the sun glistens on the leaves as they move. Ooh, look, there's a big white cloud. Maybe it's a dragon, or maybe it's a man on a magic carpet flying off to see his lover. Or they could be on a great quest. What do you see?"

Ivan shrieked again, his little legs and arms flailing about as if he wanted to touch the sky. "Oh, my precious. One day, maybe you will. Now, what else can we see."

/~/~/~/~/

Cam stumbled out of bed, dragging on his sweat pants and then rubbing the sleep out of his eyes. A quick glance through the open window let him know it was still early in the morning. The empty bed and quiet house meant Fergus was with Ivan. *Coffee. I need coffee.*

The bathroom was empty. Only a damp towel flung across the edge of the hamper letting Cam know Fergus had showered. The past five days had been hard, with both of them catnapping when they could, taking turns to respond to Ivan's yells for food. Doc said his avid feeding was all perfectly normal, given his genetics. Ivan would grow considerably faster than his human counterparts, and for that, he needed energy.

I could do with some of that energy myself, Cam thought as he ducked his head into Ivan's room. Seeing it was empty, he made his way to the kitchen. The smell of fresh coffee hit his nose and Cam's eyes gleamed spotting the full pot sitting on the element. *My mate is so good to me,* he thought as he fixed himself a cup.

Taking a long sip, Cam moved over to the kitchen window,

smiling as he caught sight of Fergus and Ivan. Fergus was clearly animated, pointing up at the sky and moving his arms around. Ivan was awake, and as he wasn't yelling, it was clear he'd been fed recently. Cam watched the chubby little legs and arms moving about, as though Ivan was telling a story too.

I am so damn lucky. Cam rubbed his chest where his heart would be. *I have a loving mate, a gorgeous son, a peaceful home and friends who care about us. I even have a mother now.* Cam thought about the long and lonely years he'd spent with a hardened heart, refusing to get close to anyone. He knew he would go through it all again, if it meant Fergus and Ivan were waiting at the end of it.

Taking another sip of his coffee, Cam gave a passing thought to Austin. *Did you do it, you old fart? Did you claim your mate or were you still determined to avoid Fate's bounty for you?* Cam realized he truly didn't care. In the end, the Fates were never wrong, and they were never thwarted either. Either Austin accepted his mate, and was now appreciating the joys of mated life, or he was dead, as his mate would be too, their souls floating wherever they went, waiting for another chance on earth to find that special love again. Together. Cam chuckled as he thought about it. Austin would find, in this life or the next, that the Fates knew him better than anyone else living could. *Maybe I'll give him a call sometime and see if he answers.*

Glancing out of the window, he could see Fergus was still talking to their son. Whereas once, Cam would have looked upon a happy scene like that and moved away, now he found himself setting his coffee mug on the bench and heading for the door. *I wonder what whimsical things I'll find in the clouds today,* he thought as he stepped outside and went to join his loving mate and son. Life honestly couldn't get any better than it was in that moment.

The End

Of course, this isn't the end of the Arrowtown series, especially with people like Rocky and Mal, and the wonderful Brutus still hoping for their own HEA one day. But Cam has always been speaking to me since book one – very quiet, I didn't know a lot about him, but I came to love him all the more while I was writing this story, and I hope you did to.

There is so much more coming up – perhaps most notably, Wesley's story from Cloverleah. I know, I have been putting it off and putting it off, mostly because it will be the last book in the series and I truly love those guys. But, my first Cloverleah book was published in February five years ago and I am determined that Wesley's story will be published on the sixth anniversary of that day. So, look for that in February (2020). I am also hoping that Baby's story from the Gods series will be out next, and if I can squeeze it in before February, the next story in the City Dragon's series. But as I am in the process of trying to buy a new house as well, we will have to see what happens.

You know, it wasn't always easy writing this story. I loved Fergus's rainbow attitude to life and people – a state of mind that's not easy to maintain if you read the news. But as

Fergus said, it's all about choice and I for one choose to maintain a positive attitude. Love will always prevail against hate.

Can you spare me a review please? I love going on the sales pages and seeing the lovely comments you share about my work. They can keep me smiling all day, and not to mention reviews are truly helpful in gaining me new readers for my story, and in uncertain financial times that is hugely helpful to me. Writing is, and has been for five years, my sole source of income and I thank everyone of you for your purchase.

Share your smile, share the love, and remember to hug the ones you love.

Lisa xx.

P.S. – Did you love the idea for those bacon and banana muffins that Brutus made? You can find the recipe for them

here -
https://www.goodtoknow.co.uk/recipes/banana-and-bacon-muffins - let me know if you try them out, my contact details are on the next page.

About the Author

Lisa Oliver lives in the wilds of New Zealand, sharing her home with her two Rotty dogs, Zeus and Hades. They can often be found, sleeping around her office chair as she taps out the stories she loves. With over sixty paranormal MM (and MMM) titles to her name so far, she shows no signs of slowing down.

When Lisa is not writing, she is usually reading with a cup of tea always at hand. Her grown children and grandchildren sometimes try and pry her away from the computer and have found that the best way to do it is to promise her chocolate. Lisa will do anything for chocolate.

Lisa loves to hear from her readers and other writers (I really do, lol). You can catch up with her on any of the social media links below.

Facebook –
http://www.facebook.com/lisaoliverauthor

Official Author page –
https://www.facebook.com/LisaOliverManloveAuthor/

My new private teaser group -
https://www.facebook.com/groups/540361549650663/

My MeWe Group -
http://mewe.com/join/lisa_olivers_paranormal_pack

And Instagram -
https://www.instagram.com/lisa_oliver_author/

My blog -
(http://www.supernaturalsmut.com)

Twitter –
http://www.twitter.com/wisecrone333

Email me directly at
yoursintuitively@gmail.com.

Other Books By Lisa/Lee Oliver

Please note, I have now marked the books that contain mpreg and MMM for those of you who don't like to read those type of stories. Hope that helps ☺

Cloverleah Pack

Book 1 – The Reluctant Wolf – Kane and Shawn

Book 2 – The Runaway Cat – Griff and Diablo

Book 3 – When No Doesn't Cut It – Damien and Scott

Book 3.5 – Never Go Back – Scott and Damien's Trip and a free story about Malacai and Elijah

Book 4 – Calming the Enforcer – Troy and Anton

Book 5 – Getting Close to the Omega – Dean and Matthew

Book 6 – Fae for All – Jax, Aelfric and Fafnir (M/M/M)

Book 7 – Watching Out for Fangs –Josh and Vadim

Book 8 – Tangling with Bears – Tobias, Luke and Kurt (M/M/M)

Book 9 – Angel in Black Leather – Adair and Vassago

Book 9.5 – Scenes from Cloverleah – four short stories featuring the men we've come to love

Book 10 – On the Brink – Teilo, Raff and Nereus (M/M/M)

Book 11 – Don't Tempt Fate – Marius and Cathair

Book 12 – My Treasure to Keep – Thomas and Ivan

Book 13 – is on the list to be written – it will be about Wesley and yes, he will find his mate too, but that's all I can say about this one for now ☺ (Coming in February 2020 - guaranteed)

The Gods Made Me Do It (Cloverleah spin off series)

Book One - Get Over It – Madison and Sebastian's story

Book Two - You've Got to be Kidding – Poseidon and Claude (mpreg)

Book Three – Don't Fight It – Lasse and Jason

Book Four – Riding the Storm – Thor and Orin (mpreg elements [Jason from previous book gives birth in this one])

Book Five – I Can See You – Artemas and Silvanus (mpreg elements – Thor gives birth in this one)

Book Six – Someone to Hold Me – Hades and Ali (mpreg elements but no birth)

The Necromancer's Smile (This is a trilogy series under the name The Necromancer's Smile where the main couple, Dakar and Sy are the focus of all three books – these cannot be read as standalone).

Book One – Dakar and Sy – The Meeting

Book Two – Dakar and Sy – Family affairs

Book Three – Dakar and Sy – Taking Care of Business

Bound and Bonded Series

Book One – Don't Touch – Levi and Steel

Book Two – Topping the Dom – Pearson and Dante

Book Three – Total Submission – Kyle and Teric

Book Four – Fighting Fangs – Ace and Devin

Book Five – No Mate of Mine – Roger and Cam

Book Six – Undesirable Mate – Phillip and Kellen

Stockton Wolves Series

Book One – Get off My Case – Shane and Dimitri

Book Two – Copping a Lot of Sin – Ben, Sin and Gabriel (M/M/M)

Book Three – Mace's Awakening – Mace and Roan

Book Four – Don't Bite – Trent and Alexi

Book Five – Tell Me the Truth – Captain Reynolds and Nico (mpreg)

Alpha and Omega Series

Book One – The Biker's Omega – Marly and Trent

Book Two – Dance Around the Cop – Zander and Terry

Book Three – Change of Plans - Q and Sully

Book Four – The Artist and His Alpha – Caden and Sean

Book Five – Harder in Heels – Ronan and Asaph

Book Six – A Touch of Spring – Bronson and Harley

Book Seven – If You Can't Stand the Heat – Wyatt and Stone (Previously published in an anthology)

Book Eight – Fagin's Folly – Fagin and Cooper

Book Nine – The Cub and His Alphas – Daniel, Zeke and Ty (MMM)

Book Ten – The One Thing Money Can't Buy – Cari and Quaid

Book Eleven – Precious Perfection – Devyn and Rex

Spin off from The Biker's Omega – BBQ, Bikes, and Bears – Clive and Roy

There will be more A&O books – This is my go-to series when I want to have fun.

Balance – Angels and Demons

The Viper's Heart – Raziel and Botis

Passion Punched King – Anael and Zagan

(Uriel and Haures's story will be coming soon)

Arrowtown

A Tiger's Tale – Ra and Seth (mpreg)

Snake Snack – Simon and Darwin (mpreg)

Liam's Lament – Liam Beau and Trent (MMM) (Mpreg)

Doc's Deputy – Deputy Joe and Doc (Mpreg)

Cam's Chance – Cam and Fergus (Mpreg) (You just read it)

NEW Series – City Dragons

Dragon's Heat – Dirk and Jon

Dragon's Fire – Samuel and Raoul

Dragon's Tears – (coming soon)

Standalone:

Rowan and the Wolf – Rowan and Shadow (series to be determined by reader vote)

Bound by Blood – Max and Lyle – (a spin off from Cloverleah Pack #7)

The Power of the Bite – Dax and Zane

One Wrong Step – Robert and Syron

Uncaged – Carlin and Lucas (Shifter's Uprising in conjunction with Thomas Oliver)

Also under the penname Lee Oliver

Northern States Pack Series

Book One – Ranger's End Game – Ranger and Aiden

Book Two – Cam's Promise – Cam and Levi

Book Three – Under Sean's
Protection – Sean and Kyle –
(Coming soon)